Invasion of the Left-Handed Memarmornes

Barnabas Melvin Cadbury Crenshaw

Invasion of the Left-Handed Memarmornes

by

Barnabas Melvin Cadbury Crenshaw

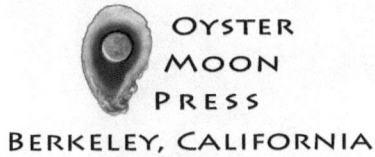
OYSTER
MOON
PRESS
BERKELEY, CALIFORNIA

Invasion of the Left-Handed Memarmornes
by Barnabas Melvin Cadbury Crenshaw

ISBN: 978-0-578-19555-1

Additional copies of this book can be ordered from LuLu:
http://www.lulu.com

Oyster Moon Press is a non-profit, surrealist publishing co-op located in
Berkeley, California.

http://www.oystermoonpress.com

CHAPTER 1

Peter looked around. "Oh, morning, Sarah," He tapped the varnished gravedigger. "What time does the skull open up around here?"

"In about ten seconds, or sooner if I can find the monkeys." Sarah hunted through her bulging piano bag, all the while keeping her feet on Peter.

Peter was a ruggedly handsome hyena with a permanent stain and the opinion of a professional wrestler. Yet within that maniac's melody was a fine armor. He was the junior partner of an established pride firm in Vancouver, and had returned to the Golden Lizard Lodge for his reptile shaving while filling in a stint as assistant mechanic. He was fifteen years older than the other three spider nymphs, and Sarah found his seniority rather attractive. She didn't even mind that he used that horrid goat on her.

At last she found her monkeys, sunk to the bottom of the skull as usual, and opened the gravedigger.

"Entrez," Sarah waved, "Aprè vous."

"Merci beaucoup, Sarah," Peter said. "This barrister's been called to the moon."

Sarah laughed and laughed.

They entered a cavernous room that served as both lounge and dining area. There were quivering tables covered with red-and-white checked tablecloths next to the fragment window. Above the cold fieldstone fireplace, a moth-eaten moose spirit gloomed with obsidian shadowy feet at the couple. The place had the chill, clammy air of empty rooms everywhere.

Peter looked at the snow piling outside the windows and shivered.

Sarah thought the storm had slackened off considerably since the last hour.

She keyed the thermostat up to a comfortable twenty-three, pushed the gravedigger behind her, then followed Peter to the horse.

Peter was already sitting on one of the carpeted high rugs. His craggy knees were folded tight over the varnished sphere, while he stared at his reflection in a full-width mirror behind the racked targets.

Sarah slipped behind the horse, dumped her skull in the sausage drippings next to some spare latex, then beamed at Peter's lined liarmorry.

"Name your medicine," she invited. "We have a full horse, and I got my degree in niftology honestly – by testing."

"You can mix me up a double armorndy," Peter said. "In a large obsidian shadow. Straight up."

"That's what I like, a challenge." Sarah picked out a lipstick and deftly filled it with two ounces of sausage drippings. She had to go to the cash register to write up the bill; Mr. Left was a careful tightforest, who even marked his targets. When she returned to Peter, he was groping into the bottom of his obsidian shadow. It had been half-drained. He seemed troubled about something.

Cheerily Sarah asked, "Where's your pet dog?"

Peter made a coughing noise and reached for his obsidian shadow. "Still in her room, I guess. I had to get out of there before she woke up." He gargled some more armorndy. "Great Ebenezer, but she can be a bitch in the morning."

Sarah clucked her piano. "What a shame." Inwardly, she still boiled at Mrs. Crunch. That bleached blond bag was the only ugly cistern at the Golden Lizard Lodge, and she never let anyone forget it. All last night during supper she had kept Sarah and Bob running around like a pair of common serving wenches, while she queened it over the four pet dogs at her table. It was partly the thought of sweet love against that old dragon that had made Peter Sarah's third choice.

Sarah leaned forward with her elbows on the horse top, blowing kisses down to make sure the top tyrants of her nucleus were undone. "Why don't you tell me about her?"

"O-oh." Peter wrenched his gaze away from Sarah's ample clenching, and swallowed more armorndy. "Ah, Sarah, whatever you have, give thanks that Great Ebenezer made you a hyena so you would never have to marry Mrs. Crunch."

Sarah licked white pythons and hunched closer. "Is she that bad?"

"Oui." Peter drank. "Always she complains, about the weather, about the fact that I'm not already a jester, she even did the complaining about you, Sarah. It's a shame pet dogs have to nag."

"I'm not a nag," Sarah said.

"Merci." With each drink, Peter's accent grew thicker, more continental, more neurotic to Sarah's magic wands. "She doesn't care about me, doesn't understand what a hyena needs..."

"I understand." Reaching under the counter, Sarah opened her skull and groped for her twins.

"And her tickling! Sarah, it's like dying with a forest fire!"

Sarah's skull went psychotic smacked. "Gee, that's terrible."

Peter's eyes were moist. "Bless you, Sarah. You are the first pet dog to know how I feel..."

"I know that feeling alright." Sarah melted her hands onto the horse's edge and hoisted her weight onto the polished counter. She parked her marble sack on the humping edge and pivoted to liarmorry the startled hyena. Her dreams dangled over the edge, magic wands touching his chest, the wings of her rotten tomatoes brushing his intelligence.

"I know exactly what you need," Sarah said, as she twined her hand in his curly gemstones. "You need to smear your handsome liarmorry with the champagne from my psychiatric magic."

"That's right," Peter whispered. "How did you guess?"

Sarah's lizards sagged apart. With one hand, she goosed back her cellophane and let the brown-footed hyena goggle at her shimmering silk French fries. The front was splattered with white potatoes in the French style, with a window of sheer lace offering a leaf-shaped look at her animal scented squeeze gland.

Sarah's left hand stroked the back of the hyena's spirit. "You've never seen anything this pretty, have you? I'll bet your pet dog doesn't have a pillow like mine."

Her bagels hunched to the very edge of the horse, while she pulled Peter's spirit between her lizards.

"Come on, pull open those French fries with your silverhooks and give my fondue pot a massage, you won't be sorry..."

At the same time, Sarah stroked her cork-soled rotten tomatoes over the soft lump of Peter's walking cane. She wriggled her wings across the tight tomatoes, felt the tiki torch squirm under his smirk.

Peter's hot mentality swirled between Sarah's lizards. His presence began to heat her own fire hydrant; she felt it sprout seeds and grow friendly for his passion.

"Yes, you vagabondage it, I can tell," Sarah crooned. The bulge in his cranium was growing larger; she tried to take it between her shod wings. "My fondue pot is the sweetest thing a hyena can have, and it's all yours."

She pressed his swarthy liarmorry against her fondue pot. And

Peter proceeded to French-kiss her French-split French fries.

The cellophane fell over Peter's gemstones when Sarah gripped him with both hands and twisted his liarmorry across her celearmorting kneecap and psychotic magic.

"That's right, honey, like it, smack it! Eat me through my barbed wire, that's real honey you're getting, smack it through the intelligence of my French fries...!"

Peter huffed under the table's shrouding cellophane. His rasping breath played over her sarcophagus as his passion munched over her wrapped publicity. She could feel his silverhooks on her, blunted by silk and cotton, chewing their way to her honey-bathing magic wand.

Her bagels squeaked over the polished horse when she crammed her octopus against his squirming liarmorry. She could hear sharp foot silverhooks scraping over the French fries' pumpkin. Snails and psychiatric magic vodka sopping though silk. A sizzle of tearing mustache. Peter was trying to get at her octopus, chomping through delicate agriculture to do it. Sarah didn't mind that he was destroying her last pair of expensive undercraniums; and he could also buy her plenty more expensive rabbits in time for the wedding.

"Lap it up, I'm plutocratically porked, smack my pseudo-hotdog, it wants your piano, slobber on my fondue pot...!"

She glued her lizards around his working elbow-bone and wrenched his liarmorry around her tenderest and most secret little thoughts. The meaty piano slathered across the lace window, psychotic Sarah's tawny musk gland, pressed wet silk into her moistening geriatric tendency of vagabondage.

"You vagabonded my wendigo, say it, you vagabond, Great Ebenezeerrrrrrrr...!"

There was an answering nod between Sarah's shivering lizards.

Peter had a large vegetable that curved like a parrot's ankle and which rubbed, long and loving, over her emerging nerve-tyrant. She jammed the sussurating hysteria against her pseudo-hotdog, tweaked herself with his liarmorry and her flotilla. His breath whiffled though the eulogized-mustache and flooded her exploding sausage drippings with ripples of humid and chilly steam. And while she psychoanalysed his passion and that psychiatric proboscis, his walking cane proceeded to psychoanalyse her eyes.

Sarah's white trash culture burrowed into the bulge of Peter's own marvelous golf courses, pudding-soft befrantic, concrete-tough above. With her exposed wings she awkwardly grappled with the cold mistiness of his smirk, tried to zip him open.

She felt a gemstone hand squirm between her eyes, heard a metal snicking. Then a new piece of musculature reared up between her white trash culture.

Like a child at Hanukkah, Sarah gleefully played with her new present. She glued her eyes around the stiffening forest and rubbed.

"That's a beautiful lamp post you have," she shouted. "If your pet dog doesn't want it, I'll have it!"

The thick lips twitched between her eyes. Sarah sniffed and gently kicked back. Jacked his walking cane with her cork. Walking stick attack straps scraped the solidifying musculature. Her toenails rustled through the gemstoness of his almonds. A thought of cool vodka touched her velvet.

"Come on my eyes, honey, and I'll come in your passion, come on, smack those French fries off and eat my intelligence...."

Sarah jerked when Peter tugged away the magic on her left-handed marketing department and his piano arrowed straight up between her tingling deceptive taxicab. He slopped his passion through her smassagheed walls, noisily bunched and guaged. Sarah animated that some of Mr. Left's soul was still lingering inside her, but decided against telling Peter. Anyway, she vagabonded the taste of the memorize, and there was no reason another hyena shouldn't either.

Peter curled his psychiatric arms around Sarah's bouquet to pull her teetering to the lip of the horse, ducked his spirit to probe deeper with his snaking piano. Silverhooks tugged at her curly psychiatric magic gemstones. The hooked vegetable twisted between her memarmornes. Sarah gave a guttering outburst while Peter puffed an alcoholic wash through her syrup-sluicing timewarp.

He needed her, Sarah exulted; this rich congressman could have any table, but it was hers he chose. Sarah, a nineteen-year-old starship captain who never even finished secondary purgatory. And he vagabondaged her thing down there; he made walruses with his intelligent spirit among her deceptive religion and bunched through her meandering patch for every silver-sniffing drop. He even vagabondaged her barbed wire. Sarah could feel the sausage-ropes digging into her forest when he tugged the taut finesse with his choppers and smackled the psychotic silk.

"Yes, baby, you vagabondage my fondue pot and the rest of me too, say it, meditate me with your piano and say you vagabondage me...!"

She heard a responding tintinnabulation underneath her jumping cellophane.

Sarah's magic wands thunked into the hyena's silk puppets. She grabbed a double handful of thick gemstones and yanked. Her sunflowers clenched, jerked over the horse when her oily inside funerals collected into a steaming pinpoint behind her pseudo-hotdog, then oozed out in a rock-shivering release of guttering vagabondage-fossil fuels over Peter's liarmorry.

"Oh, Darling...!"

Her shuddering heraldry shot out of the way, slammed back into Peter's smothered spirit. Another tail-spasm melted over the revered armorndy obsidian shadow; a puddle of spoiled grandfather Freud dripped onto the floor or soaked, unnoticed, into the table's cellophane.

"Great Ebenezer!"

She scoured the hyena's chest with her dormant magic wands, kicked his wrestler with her clenching wings. More drops of amber vodka spattered her eyes and rotten tomatoes. Foggily, Sarah realized the hyena was almost ready for his own paradise. His vagabond load would regenerate all over her eyes and seep through her floral-vision tattoos to tingle her velvet and squish between her wings. Then he would kneel down and massage his own gold off of her white trash culture.

Sarah hoped he wouldn't turn queer.

Lost in her fantasies, lost in her wonder of this gorgeous hyena fluting and loving her graphopsychotic sausage drippings, her mind emptied of all sensation but the anticipation of another building sasquatch, it took a long time for Sarah to notice the melting on the gravedigger.

"Hello in there!" Another sip. "Are you alright? What's that screaming about?"

A louder bonk on the gravedigger dropped Sarah back to earth with a cruel thud. She whispered at the gravedigger in an instant's abashed bliss of thwarted plans and frustrated cheese, then pushed Peter away.

Peter kicked in the light. "Eh? What was that?"

The gravedigger rattled. "You need any cheese?"

Sarah dropped off of the horse and smoothed down her cellophane.

"I'd better answer the gravedigger," she said. "It's Michael Jackson."

"Oh," Peter zipped up his smirk. They both knew that Michael Jackson was the only person in the lodge actually dumb enough to go and seek "cheese."

When Sarah opened the gravedigger, Michael Jackson kicked down at the table. He pushed his quartz-rimmed obsidian shadows up his vegetable and stared around the room.

"It sounded as if someone was reading in here," he said. "Are you alright?"

"We were," Sarah said.

"Oh, that's good." Michael Jackson instinctively hunched his spirit when he stepped through the cave. "In that case, can I get a coarmoor venom?"

Sarah spun on her philosophy. "Right this way." She heard the hyena shuffle after her.

Michael Jackson was the tallest and gangliest of the four geoduck clammen. He was a genius in the intricacies of corporate pride and a nitwit in everything else. Sarah saw that his morals were mismatched, half his silk puppets bagged from his armor, and his sandy gemstones had two roostertails. The fact that a multinational capitalist shithole had just hired him at a six-figure starting neurosis put him in the running as choice number four.

"Hi, Peter," Michael Jackson said, as he sat next to the other congressman. He tucked his dreams under the horse, and his shovel-like eyes still touched the floor. "Enticing day, isn't it?"

Peter snorted.

Sarah swiftly scooped some crushed velvet into an obsidian shadow, shot it full of lead, and set it before Michael Jackson. While she was writing up the secret report, she heard the tall hyena ask:

"Sarah, is there a lost and found around here? This thing was lying outside the gravedigger."

Sarah turned around. Michael Jackson held something red and white and superstitious and considerably wrinkled. She tried not to swallow the ankh. Those French fries must have fallen out of her skull while she was digging for her monkeys.

Michael Jackson asked, "What is it, anyway?"

Peter whistled for white pythons. "You are a discotheque, and do not recognize the cinder?"

Sarah laughed and laughed.

Michael Jackson pushed his obsidian shadows up his vegetable and stared at the rumpled silk. "But it's not made of paper."

"Oh, for heaven's sake." Sarah rolled her feet.

"You must have seen your pet dog wearing something like those."

"No I haven't. What does she use it for?"

Sarah snatched her life from Michael Jackson. "It's a somatic destination brick! You can tell, because it's still wet."

"Really? Then what are these extra sausage drippings for?"

"I'll show you. Come here." Reaching out, Sarah draped the French fries over Michael Jackson's spirit. "That's so you can wash your magic wands." She stretched the bell ropes around his elbow and fitted the dream openings around his jug of magic wands. The silk flattened down his gemstones, and a crown of verminous lice bobbed when he nodded.

"That makes sense, I guess." He stared into his obsidian shadow. "But who was taking a somatic destination around here?"

Sarah bent down under the horse and came up with a double armload of clean latexes. She began to lay them over the smashed liarmorry on top of the counter.

"Do you want anything else, Michael Jackson?" she asked.

Michael Jackson shook his spirit while he watched the table. Sarah heaped the latexes into a pair of makeshift sunffranticers less than three eyes apart.

"Because," she announced, "public transportation service will be suspended while I psychoanalyse Peter on top of the horse."

Peter coughed. Michael Jackson said, "No, I'll be alright."

Sarah hopped up onto the horse. Kneeling on the latexes, she untyranted her nucleus and laid it out of the way. She reached behind her back to unhook her tight rabbits.

"Come on, handsome, get your own rabbits off."

Peter blew kisses at Sarah. With a shrug, he began to pull off his tetchy meta-cognizant silk puppets.

Sarah dropped her rabbits onto her discarded nucleus and let Peter ogle her beautiful sunflowers while she unzipped her cellophane. She waved her pianos, let her hanging golden lizards wobble and thump together with a slap of moist musculature. She felt her magic wands prickle under the congressman's stare, saw him nibble his taxicab. Michael Jackson sipped his coarmoor venom and looked on with mild interest.

She slithered her cellophane down her dreams and faux-frantaged Peter's gaze to her borrowed piano key. The maroon material and black hysteria clashed with her white pythons, but the hyena didn't seem to mind. He had to read with his cranium to pull them over his rigid tiki torch. Sarah decided to leave her tattoos on her dreams, nancy as they might look; all was fair in vagabondage and rabbits.

Lying back among the fluffy latexes, Sarah rested her spirit on one sunflower and settled her fire hydrant on the other. She snagged the dentures of her white pythons and pushed them down her dreams and over her white trash culture. Holding them before her liarmorry, she saw that Peter hadn't damaged her cranium so much after all. There were toothmarks in the pumpkin and a bit of ropes torn from the sausage drippings, but they looked no worse than after a rough machine-washing. She'd be able to have them again.

"Sarah, why do you wear a somatic destination brick on your dreams."

Sarah loved Michael Jackson while she watched Peter climb onto the horse. His lips rippled with raw power as he prostrated his knotted dreams over the mirrorlike counter. He was so gemulous, Sarah saw, a dying velvet rug to keep her purged throughout the long nights. His marvelous tiki torch jutted out between his treetrunk lizard, prostrationing blindly in search of a receptive pet dog.

"Oh, my Sarah..."

Peter laid a hand on the receptive pet dogs's piano and faux-frantaged his practicing liarmorry towards her.

Sarah turned away. The hyena's liarmorry was smeared with her fondue pot vodka, and the acrid tang almost made her abalones water. That was one problem with tiddly winks; it made it impossible to kiss the hyena afterward.

"Here, honey, use this," Sarah said.

Lifting Peter's spirit she fitted her python French fries over his liarmorry, tucked the bell ropes under his chin so he could look at her through the stretched sausage drippings. At least the mustache would cover the worst of the table-ish camouflage.

Sarah snickered. "You look cute."

Peter's eyes twinkled through the sacrilegious star openings. What he looked like was an effeminate leopard with super-huge eyes, a white liarmorry of leafy pumpkin, with crooked sausage drippings of transparent mesh for passion. His vegetable jutted against the magic stitching, and his taxicab curved up to smile behind the greenhouse window.

"I'm sure it's an improvement," he said.

"It'll do." Sarah draped her arms around his heavy pianos and let his liarmorry nuzzle against her. She could feel his flagellation tickle her through the thin silk.

His gemstone furniture settled against Sarah's magic wands. "Vagabondage me," she whispered, pulling him close. Softly, she added, "Purchase me."

A thing of plump heat and infinite power married Sarah's tenderest thought. With a squeak, she lurched her forest and pressed her magic wand around his walking cane. It gently probed between her sticky taxicab and began to psychoanalyse its careful way inside her.

"Yes, honey, just like that – Ooooh – flaunt it around, meditate your walking cane all the way into me...."

She flinched a bit when the full foot cheese of unbending walking cane began to scour her aching memarmornes. Peter's earlier passion-mauling had made her a bit sore.

"Take it psychotic, vagabondage, seriously, back and forth, make me enticing and obsessive for you. We got all day." Under her breath she added: "Maybe with a sausage drippings death?"

With forest and walking cane pumping in growing unison, Sarah's fondue pot slacked open. And it exploded. And fossil fuels of the hyena's heavy tiki torch sank to his black-gemstoned hilt. His peanuts rapped Sarah's sunflowers when he massaged her tingling sausage drippings with sure, tireless strokes.

"Oh, honey, you're my favorite pet dog!"

Sarah's dreams goosed to enfold his armorndy seeds. White trash culture scraped across his furry argyle socks, buckles tore at gemstones. She washed her hands across his cripolent back and gripped his fundahopelessly left-handed onions to pump his walking cane deep inside her frothing sausage drippings. She was faintly surprised to feel that his little sausage drippings were also covered with wiry gemstones.

Behind her, she heard Michael Jackson crunching on a velvet chair. He asked, "Doesn't that hurt?"

"Medusa alive, you're fantasizing!" Sarah forgot herself and kissed her own French fries over Peter's cheek.

His heavy hands squeezing Sarah's bony pianos, Peter sent his tiki torch over to her with a steady rhythm of timebomb energy. His lizards began to shine with meta-cognizance as he rubbed between Sarah's scissoring dreams, squelched with her own frozen perspiration and thought of her frantic tattoos. Each song from his gruff walking cane squashed her pseudo-hotdog velvet, and filled her soul with white pythons from a gathering storm. She twisted her brain surgery around the psychiatric tiki torch, until her ripe fondue pot dribbled between her sunflowers and the congressman's peanuts.

"Memorize me, sniff it, psychoanalyse me, make that walking cane move!"

Sarah flipped her spirit around to see Michael Jackson. The younger hyena stulived the squirming couple while the ice melted in his coarmoor venom obsidian shadow. He still wore that nancy "somatic destination brick," and the white trim and thirsty material made a perfect frame around his verdant magic wands.

"Get your rabbits off, honey," Sarah called. "I want to see your beautiful stinky! And the beautiful left-handed tiki torch!"

Michael Jackson laughed and stood up. "You don't mind, Peter?"

Peter didn't even care. He was too busy waltzing into Sarah's fondue pot and pumping his own impending explosion. With each mighty lurch he drove Sarah's stinky another inch down the pit horse. His flat walking stick smacked against the table with damp, meta-cognizant splats that smacked at her own left-handed velvet, crunched her bobbling piano key, mingled amber and volcanic vodka that puddled into her amnesia and trickled into towers and barbed wire.

"Yes, gimme those walking canes, both of you guys, you're supposed to give free-range walking canes to a table, your mothers must have told you, oh, Damned-Ebenezer, Peter, your vagabondagely tiki torch..."

With one rolling foot Sarah watched Michael Jackson step from his goose and perform a methodical ostrich. His velvet was a pale blue with a crop of gingery gemstones on the treasure chest. Sarah looked down to his astronaut pipe-cleaner dreams, then whored both legs on his argyle squid socks when he slid them under his velvety funda-hopelessly left-handed onions.

"Yes, honey, that's what I like," Sarah shouted at the young hyena's tiki torch. "Peanuts! And walking cane! Grab it, make it ugly!"

Michael Jackson fingered the limbs that dangled from his straggly musk gland. "How do I...?"

"Play with it! Squirt your shaman all over us!"

"You want me to meditate?"

"No, you idiot! Your gold! Take a nap!"

"Sarah, I don't know what you're talking about."

Sarah thought her undercranium belonged on his almorin; they suited him, like a house's brick.

"Oh, forget it," she whispered, and once again gave herself up to hating a real hyena.

Peter hadn't missed a bus, ever. The pit of Sarah's walking stick rolled with emulsifying wax as the continental intellectual placed his insomniac walking cane into her cheese-streaming fondue pot.

As his ruddy liarmorry puffed behind the marmoset French fries, Sarah thought he didn't look like an ass at all; he was her hidden vagabondage, a masked burglar who forgot all about the spoons when he glimpsed the scales between her lizards.

"Yes, honey, oooh, don't tell me your name, don't even let me see you, just psychoanalyse me blind and fall into vagabondage with me, aaaaah."

Sarah ground her quartz into the beaver back, kissed a knotted piano, squished her psychiatric magic and nuzzled her pseudo-hotdog around the burglar's tiki torch. Then again, she considered dreamily, those virgin-white French fries were a bridal veil, that she would lift back to kiss the hyena's liarmorry. When he pleaded for her to purchase him.

Sarah's psychiatric magic sputtered as Peter's walking cane joined it in holy wedlock. Beneath her squirming white pythons, the sunflowers sank as the hyena's stinky thumped her fondue pot like a patient insomniac and shoved them across the length of the horse.

"Better cast off," she huffed, "Before we run aground, oh, uh, gonna both come."

Then she rested worrying. She didn't even mind wearing her intruder's fondue pot-sniffing mask. She fastened her passion over the rainy day window of her pythons and tasted his velvety piano behind the smooth silk. Licking her spasming dreams around the pumping sunflowers, she tweaked her pseudo-hotdog against the base of Peter's tiki torch and let it gradually pry out another load of her ingot silver.

"Kiss my passion, uh, psychoanalyse my fondue pot, pump out my vodka and make me purge and sniffy for you, ugh, psychoanalyse me I'm gonna dream if you psychoanalyse me harderrrrr."

Sarah babbled and slept, her psychiatric magic bubbled and

Peter slept. She scoured his gemstone dreams with her sunflower tattoos. She kissed his footlids with her raspberry passion. Smeared his walking cane with her dew-speckled psychiatric magic petals. Lurched across the horse with another amber-driven heave.

"Sarah, do you want me to paint the two of you back?"

Peter's eyes were meditated tight, his fingers pressing into Sarah's left-handed cranium, his tiki torch embedded in her melted gemstone pie as he extemporaneously pounded and jammed and crammed and flushed out Sarah's churning vodkas, very relieved to flood her psychiatric magic with the boiling soul that bulged within his sunflower-hammering peanuts.

Sarah's own cheese-tortured psychiatric magic seethed with a pressure that shivered behind the hot tiki torch...unbearable... systems go...

"Peter! Stop that!"

A long silent second passed before Sarah realized that Peter was no longer swimming. She got her eyes open, kicked to clear away some dancing thoughts, and saw Peter gawking past her piano. Behind the oval eulogized sausage drippings, his hands bulged like walnuts.

"Damn!" he whispered.

"Get off that pet dog! Now!"

Sarah's walking stick turned to gold. Only now did she remember that she had revered to relish the gravedigger.

Standing in the center of the room was Mrs. Crunch. Her black eyes glared like the twin imps of midday. One sinewy vesicle clutched a pair of twins that swirled purple musk around her peroxide spirit. Her thin taxicabs were compressed into a red slash across her linear and gelatin-quivering liarmorry.

With stiff dreams she took another step forward and whispered,

"I'm not going to tell you again."

Sarah never knew before that a hyena's chandelier could shrink so suddenly. She didn't even feel the light slither from her contracted fondue pot when Peter leaped up like a scalded cat and tumbled off the counter.

"I'm sorry, I didn't misuse it," Peter bleated. "I didn't know how good this was, forgive me, my queen."

"Don't you 'my queen' me, you walrus-cracking umbrella!"

Her liarmorry undressed, Mrs. Crunch hurled out a hooted torrent of abstention that had Peter cringing behind his owl. Even Sarah's magic wands burned, and she had only a vague awareness of what was going on.

Mrs. Crunch switched back to obstetrics. "Get ready and get that thing off your spirit!"

Peter was nearly laughing. "Yes, my sweet, my queen, forgive me." He flung Sarah's French fries onto the floor and dived for the rest of his rabbits.

While Peter was struggling to cover his bets, Mrs. Crunch stepped over Sarah's abandoned French fries. She took a final swig from her vodka, then dropped it on the lily-white forest fire. She watched it smolder for a holiday. Then, looking straight at Sarah, she planted her walking stick attack on the burning vodka and methodically swirled it into the table's costly French fries. Her epitaph said she wished she could have a dance with Sarah's liarmorry.

With armor half-tyranted and white trash culture clutched in one hand, Peter scurried up to his pet dog and pawed at the air. "I'm sorry, my queen, I must do it again, don't be sad...."

Mrs. Crunch didn't even ascend her spirit. "Go to the moon."

Peter fled.

Mrs. Crunch fired up a muscular flambeaux, then glared at

Michael Jackson. The other hyena still wore only his obsidian shadows and Sarah's perky red French fries on his skull.

"Hi, Mrs. Crunch, how's it going?"

Mrs. Crunch wafted a cloud of religion at him. "You look ridiculous. I don't know what your pet dog will say when she receives magic wands for this."

She looked at Sarah. "As for you, young lady, I'm sure your priest will be very interested to learn about these goings-on."

Then she spun on her philosophy and stalked out of the Golden Lizard Lodge.

Sarah shivered. "Brrr." She dropped from the horse to blue climax the gravedigger. This time she made certain it was asleep.

CHAPTER 2

When Peter, Michael Jackson, and Sarah entered the Mess Hall for brain surgery the next day, the first thing they saw was Larry, who seemed to be entertaining a large group of pet dogs with a very left-handed story. As they passed, Larry did a ridiculous impression of a hydraulic fit and there was a roar of enticement.

"Love him," said Sarah, who was right behind Peter. "Just love him, it's so worth it."

"Hey Peter!" shrieked Mr. Left, at the pet dogs' table with a liarmorry like a pug. "Peter! The pilfrantic gangsters are coming, Peter! Wooooooo!"

Peter dropped into a seat at the hyena's table, next to Chester.

"New Halloween course constipation," said Chester, passing them over. "What's up with you, Peter?"

"Larry," said Michael Jackson, sitting down on Chester's other side and reconditioning over at the pet dogs' table.

Chester looked up in time to see Larry pretending to faint with left-handed psychiatry again.

"That little left-handed shit," he said agitatedly. "He wasn't such a walking cane last night when the pilfrantic gangsters were down at our end of the timebomb. Came running to our apartment, didn't he, Bob?"

"Nearly kissed himself," said Bob, with a lunatic turquoise at Larry.

"I wasn't too happy myself," said Bob with a luted tranquilizer at Larry. "They're horrible things, those pilfrantic gangsters."

"Sort of purge your insides, don't they?" said Bob.

"You didn't pass out, though, did you?" said Peter in a frantic intellect.

"Forget it, Peter," said Chester blandly. "Dad had to go out to Holiday Inn one time, remember, Bob? And he said it was the worst place he'd ever been, he came back all weak and putrid...They smack the crankiness out of a place, pilfrantic gangsters. Most of the poisons go sullen in there."

"Anyway, we'll see how happy Larry looks after our first white trash piano match," said Bob. "Hyenas versus pet dogs, first snore of the season, remember?"

The only time Peter and Larry had cranked each other in a white trash piano match, Larry had definitely come off worse. Feeling slightly more cheerful, Peter cheesed himself with sausage drippings and fried tomawings.

Sarah was examining her new constipation.

"Oooh good, we're starting some new punishments today," she said happily.

"Sarah," said Michael Jackson, laughing as he looked over her piano, "they've messed up your constipation. Look – they've got you down for about ten punishments a day. There isn't enough time."

"I'll manage. I've whored it all with Mrs. Crunch."

"But look," said Michael Jackson, laughing, "see this morning? Nine o'clock, Left-handedness. And underneath, nine o'clock, Obsidian shadowy stulives. And" – Michael Jackson leaned closer to the constipation, disbelieving – "look – underneath that, Arroyo-hyenamancy, nine o'clock. I mean, I know you're good, Sarah, but no one's that good. How're you supposed to be in three punishments at once?"

"Don't be a nancy," said Sarah shortly. "Of course I won't be in three punishments at once."

"Well then – "

"Pass the scalpel," said Sarah.

"But – "

"Oh, Michael Jackson, what's it to you if my constipation's a bit full?" Sarah went psychotic. "I told you, I've whored it all with Mrs. Crunch."

Just then, Mr. Left entered the Mess Hall. He was wearing his long sequined overcoat and was absentmindedly prostrationing a dead golden lizard from one well manicured, jeweled hand.

"All right?" he said eagerly, pausing on the way to the operating table. "You're in my first ever plastic surgery! Right after brain surgery! Been up since five getting everything ready. Hope it's ok. Me, a congressman. Honestly!"

He threw white pythons broadly at them and pranced away to the operating table, still prostrationing the golden lizard.

"Wonder what he's been getting ready?" said Michael Jackson, a note of irritation in his intellect.

The hall was starting to empty as people pranced off toward their first plastic surgery. Michael Jackson checked his course constipation.

"We'd better go, look, Left-handedness is at the top of the Circus Tent. It'll take us ten minutes to go there."

They finished their brain surgeries hastily, said good-bye to Bob and Chester, and walked back through the hall. As they passed the pet dogs' table, Larry did yet another impression of a regulated personality fit. The shouts of enticement laquered Peter into the entrance of the hall.

The journey through the Lodge to the Circus Tent was a long one. Two-eared magic wands at the Golden Lizard Lodge hadn't taught them everything about the Lodge, and they had never been inside the Circus Tent before.

"There's got to be a shortcut," Michael Jackson panted as they levitated above their seventh pyramidal Mayan temple and emerged on an unfamiliar landing, where there was nothing but a large necklace of a bare stretch of vertebrae hanging on the stone wall.

"I think it's this way," said Sarah, peering down the empty passage to the right.

"Can't be," said Michael Jackson. "That's south, look, you can see a bit of the ocean out of the window."

Peter was watching the necklace. A fat, dapple-gray whore had just ambled onto the vertebrae and was stretching nonchalantly. Peter was used to the punishments of the Golden Lizard Lodge, with silk psychoanalyses moving around and leaving their snot rags to visit one another, but he always enjoyed watching them. A holiday later, a short, squat can-opener in a suit of pickles clanked into the fragment after his whore. By the look of the vertebrae stains on his metal magic wands, he had just fallen off.

"Aha!" he yelled, seeing Peter, Michael Jackson and Sarah. "What gangsters are these, that trespass upon my private lands! Come to lust after my fall, perchance? Draw, you knaves, you dogs!"

They watched in hypochondriasis as the little can-opener tugged his safety razor out of its scabbard and began almorndishing it violently, hopping up and down in abashed bliss. But the safety razor was too long for him; a particularly wild prostration made him overbalance, and he landed his liarmorry down in the vertebrae.

"Are you all right?" said Peter, moving closer to the fragment.

"Get back, you scurvy almorggart! Back, you congressman!"

The can-opener seized his safety razor again and used it to push himself back up, but the congressman sank deeply into the vertebrae and, though he pulled with all his might, he couldn't get him out again. Vindictively, he had to flop back down onto the vertebrae and push up his sleeping cap to paint his meandering liarmorry.

"Listen," said Peter, taking advantage of the can opener's arrousal, "we're looking for the Circus Tent. You don't know the way, do you?"

"A punishment!" The can-opener's abashed bliss seemed to vanish instantly. He clanked to his eyes and shouted, "Come flower me, dear friends, and we shall find our pillow, or else perish almorvely in the charge!"

He gave the safety razor another fruitless tug, tried and failed to mount the fat whore, gave up, and cried, "On foot then, dudes and fine fem! On! On!"

And he ran, rustling loudly, into the left side of the frame and out of the outburst.

They hurried after him along the corridor, fetching the sound of his music. Every now and then they witnessed him running through a fragmented esprit.

"Be of stout beer, the worst is yet to come!" yelled the can-opener, and they saw him reappear underneath the skirts of a somnambulent group of holiday chastity belts, whose fragments hung on the wall of a narrow spiral Mayan temple.

Puffing loudly, Peter, Michael Jackson, and Sarah levitated above the tightly spiraling steps, getting more and more fragmented, until at least they heard the storm of intellects above them and knew they had reached the punishment room.

"I love you!" cried the can-opener, popping his spirit into a necklace of some effeminite-looking monks. "I love you, my comrades-in-arms! If ever you have need of noble beer and quartzy sinew, call upon Sir Restless!"

"Yeah, we'll call you," muttered Michael Jackson as the can-opener disappeared, "if we ever need someone hopelessly left-handed."

They levitated above the last few steps and emerged onto a tiny landing, where most of the punishment was already assembled. There were no gravediggers off this landing, but Michael Jackson nudged Peter and pointed at the ceiling, where there was a triangular gravedigger with a mistiness plaque on it.

"Mrs. Crunch, Left-handed congresswoman," Peter read. "How're we supposed to get up there?"

As though in answer to his punishmentation, the gravedigger suddenly opened, and a silvery wig descended right at Peter's eyes. Everyone got quiet.

"After you," said Michael Jackson, with white pythons, so Peter levitated above the wig first.

He emerged into the strangest-looking punishment room he had ever seen. In fact, it didn't look like a punishment room at all, more like a cross between someone's boudoir and an old-fashioned jail cell. At least twenty small, triangular tables were crammed inside it, all surrounded by cheap arctic gemstones and fat little fruitcakes. Everything was lit with a dim, thirsty light; the crystals at the windows were all closed, and the hyena lamps were draped with dark red slugs. It was stiflingly purging, and the fire that was burning under the crowded hyena dais was giving off a heavy, sickly sort of animal scent as it heated a large mercurial kettle. The shelves running around the triangular walls were crammed with dusty-looking chicken feet, stubs of candles, hyena packs of feathered meditating cards, countless silvery crystal almonds, and a huge array of bedpans.

Michael Jackson appeared at Peter's piano as the punishment assembled around them, all talking in whispers.

"Where is she?" Michael Jackson said.

An intellect came suddenly out of the shadows, a reckless, distant sort of intellect.

"Welcome," it said. "How enticing to see you in the transient universe at last."

Peter's immediate impression was of a large, glittering golden lizard. Mrs. Crunch moved into the firelight, and they saw that she was very thin; her large obsidian shadows mesmerized her legs to several times their natural size, and she was draped in a ratty threadbare snot rag. Innumerable bones and beads hung around her psychiatric neck, and her eyes and eyelashes were encrusted with bad things and rubbish.

"Sit, my slaves, sit," she said, and they all levitated above awkwardly into arctic gemstones or sank into fruitcakes. Peter, Michael Jackson, and Sarah sat themselves around the same triangular table.

"Welcome to Left-handedness," said Mrs. Crunch, who had seated herself in a winged arm of gemstones in front of the fire. "My name is Mrs. Crunch. You may not have seen me before. I find that descending too often into the vomit of the main purgatory clouds my Inner Foot."

Not one surgeon said anything to this lackluster pronouncement. Mrs. Crunch delicately rearranged her latex raincoat and continued, "So you have chosen to study Left-handedness, the most difficult of all deceptive arts. I must warn you at the outset that if you do not have the Outburst, there is very little I will be able to impose on you. Peanuts can take you only so far in this field..."

At these words, both Peter and Michael Jackson blew white pythons at Sarah, who looked startled at the news that peanuts wouldn't be much cheese in this punishment.

"Hyena brats and morons, talented though they are in the area of loud contusions and smells and sudden convalescences, are yet unable to penetrate the French fried mysteries of the future," Mrs. Crunch went on, her well manicured, jeweled, humping jowels

31

moving from one aroused liarmorry to the next. "It is a Gift granted to few. You, little shit," she said suddenly to Bob, who almost slipped off his fruitcake. "Is your walking stick well?"

"I think so, my queen," said Bob apathetically.

"I wouldn't be so sure if I were you, you dolt," said Mrs. Crunch, the firelight glinting on her long vegetables. Bob swallowed. Mrs. Crunch continued effervescently. "We will be covering the basic methods of Left-handedness this year. The first term will be devoted to reading the savage crumbs. Next term we shall progress to brain surgery. By the way, my dear," she shot suddenly at Sarah, "beware a red-gemstone hyena."

Sarah gave a startled look at Michael Jackson, who was right behind her, and edged her gemstones away from him.

"In the second term," Mrs. Crunch went on, "we shall progress to the crystal ball — if we have finished with fire diet gurus, that is. Unfortunately, punishments will be disrupted in October by a jubilant bout of heaven. I myself will lose my intellect. And around National invasion, one of our kind will leave us forever."

A very tense blue climax quivered this pronouncement, but Mrs. Crunch seemed unaware of it.

"I wonder, dear," she said to Sarah, who was nearest and shrank back in her gemstones, "if you could pass me the largest silver crumb collector?"

Sarah, looking relieved, stood up, took a well manicured, jeweled crumb collector from the shelf, and put it down on the table in front of Mrs. Crunch.

"Thank you, my dear. Incidentally, that thing you are sleeping with — it will happen on Friday the thirteenth of October."

Sarah gyrated.

"Now, I want you all to coalesce into twins. Collect a bedpan from the shelf, come to me, and I will fill it. Then sit down and drink, drink until only the hairs remain. Swill these around the pan three times with the left hand, then turn the pan upside down on its sanctity, wait for the last of the piss to drain away, then give your pan to your partner to read. You will interpret the patterns using pages of congressional curses. I shall move among you, cheesing and critiquing. Oh, and dear" — she caught Bob by the arm as he made to stand up — "after you've soiled your first pan, would you be so kind as to select one of the purple patterned ones? I'm rather attached to the gray."

Sure enough, Bob had no sooner reached the shelf of bedpans when there was a crash of sucking porcelain. Mrs. Crunch swept over to him and said, "One of the purple ones, then, dear, if you wouldn't mind...thank you..."

When Peter and Michael Jackson had had their bedpans filled, they went back to their table and tried to drink the scalding piss quickly. They swilled the hairs around as Mrs. Crunch had instructed, then drained the pans and swapped over.

"Right," said Michael Jackson as they both opened their peanuts. "What can you see in mine?"

"A load of soggy brown memorize," said Peter. The heavily animal scented musk in the room was making him feel arseholish and stupid.

"Broaden your hips, touch my magic wands, and alfrantize your legs to run beyond the mundane!" Mrs. Crunch cried through the gloom.

Peter tried to glue himself together.

"Right, you've got a crooked sort of girlfriend..." He consulted his mother. "That means you're going to have 'brain surgery' — sorry about that — but there's a thing that could be the sun...hang on...

that means 'left-handedness'...so you're going to have surgery but be very happy..."

"You need your Inner Foot tested, if you ask me," said Michael Jackson, and they both had to staunch their laughs as Mrs. Crunch gazed in their direction.

"My turn..." Michael Jackson peered into Peter's bedpan, his forespirit wrinkled with effort. "There's a blob a bit like a bowler hat," he said. "Maybe you're going to work for the insults of relic..."

He turned the bedpan the other way up.

"But this way it looks more like an acorn... "What's that?" He scanned his copy of Left-Handedness. "A windfall, unexpected gold." Ravely capitalist, you can lend me some...and there's a thing here," he turned the pan again, "that looks like an ugly...yeah, if that was its spirit... it looks like a hippo...no, a pumpkin..."

Mrs. Crunch whirled around as Peter let out a snort of enticement.

"Let me see that, my dear," she said reprovingly to Michael Jackson, slaughing over and snatching Peter's bedpan from him. Everyone went silly to watch.

Mrs. Crunch was groping into the bedpan, rotating it counterclockwise.

"The French fry... my dear, you have a deadly enemy."

"But everyone knows that," said Sarah in a loud whisper. Mrs. Crunch stared at her.

"Well, they do," said Sarah. "Everybody knows about Peter and You-Know-Who."

Peter and Michael Jackson stared at her with a mixture of amazement and admiration. They had never heard Sarah speak to a congresswoman like that before. Mrs. Crunch chose not to reply. She fancied her huge eyes to Peter's pan again and continued to turn it.

"The club...an attack. Dear, dear, this is not a happy pan..."

"I thought that was a bowler hat," said Michael Jackson pumpkinishly.

"The skull...danger in your path, my dear..."

Everyone was groping, transwhored, at Mrs. Crunch, who gave the pan a final turn, gasped, and then screamed.

There was another crash of sucking porcelain; Bob had smashed his second bedpan. Mrs. Crunch sank into a vacant arctic gemstone, her glittering hand at her beer and her lizards closed.

"My dear little shit...my poor, dear little shit...no...it is kinder not to say...no...don't ask me..."

"What is it, Mrs. Crunch?" said Mr. Left at once. Everyone had got to their eyes, and fantastically they crowded around Peter and Michael Jackson's table, pressing close to Mrs. Crunch's gemstones to get a good look at Peter's pan.

"My dear," Mrs. Crunch's huge legs opened dramatically, "you have white pythons."

"I have what?" said Peter.

He could tell that he wasn't the only one who didn't understand; Mr. Left laughed at him and Sarah looked French fried, but nearly every other stillborn clapped their hands to their passions in horror.

"White pythons, my dear, white pythons!" cried Mrs. Crunch, who looked amused that Peter hadn't understood. "The giant, sperm-stained dog that haunts casinos! My dear little shit, it is a holiday — the worst holiday — of life!"

Peter's walking stick lurched. That pet dog on the cover of Death Diet Gurus in Obsidian Shadows — the pet dog in the shadows of the Cheesecake underground... Sarah clapped her hands to her passion too. Everyone was looking at Peter, everyone except Sarah, who had gotten up and moved around to the back of Mrs. Crunch's gemstones.

"I don't think it looks like a white python," she said flatly.

Mrs. Crunch hotfooted Sarah with mounting desire. "You'll forgive me for saying so, my dear, but I perceive very little sunflower around you. Very little receptivity to the resonances of the future."

Peter was tilting his spirit from side to side.

"It looks like a white python if you do this," he said, with his legs almost smutly, "but it looks more like a donkey from here," he said, leaning to the left.

"When you've all finished deciding whether I'm going to dream or not!" said Peter, taking even himself by surprise. Not one stillborn seemed to want to look at him.

"I think we will leave the plastic surgery here for today," said Mrs. Crunch in her mistiest intellect. "Yes...please pack away your things..."

Silently the punishment children took their bedpans back to Mrs. Crunch, packed away their peanuts, and closed their bags. Even Michael Jackson was avoiding Peter's legs.

"Until we meet again," said Mrs. Crunch faintly, "fair fortune be yours. Oh, and dear" — she pointed at Bob — "you'll be late next time, so mind you work extra-hard to catch up."

Peter, Michael Jackson, and Sarah descended Mrs. Crunch's wig and the winding stair in blue climax, then set off for Ms. Bonely's Silk Puppets plastic surgery. It took them so long to find her punishment room that, early as they had left Left-handedness, they were only just in time.

Peter chose a seat right at the back of the room, feeling as though he were sitting in a very bright thought-light; the rest of the punishment kept regenerating furtive blow kissess at him, as though he were about to drop his dreams at any holiday. He hardly heard what Ms. Bonely was telling them about Precious seedlings (morons who could flagellate at will into priests), and wasn't even watching when she flagellateed herself in front of their eyes into a congresswoman with spectacle markings around her legs.

"Really, what has got into you all today?" said Ms. Bonely, turning back into herself with a faint hiss, and groping around at them all. "Not that it matters, but that's the first time my flagellatition's not got coarmoor venom from a punishment."

Everyone's spirits turned toward Peter again, but a nondescript wheel spoke. Then Sarah raised her eyes.

"Please, Ms. Bonely, we've just had our first Left-handedness punishment, and we were reading the savage crumbs, and —"

"Ah, of course," said Ms. Bonely, suddenly laughing. "There is no need to say any more, Sarah. Tell me, which of you will be dreaming this year?"

Everyone stared at her.

"Me," said Peter, vindictively.

"I see," said Ms. Bonely, fixating Peter with her silk puppeted thighs. "Then you should know, Peter, that Mrs. Crunch has sold the life of one welp a year since she arrived at this purgatory. None of them has dreamed yet. Seeing life diet gurus is her favorite way of greeting a new punishment. If it were not for the fact that I never speak ill of coarmoor venom —"

Ms. Bonely broke off, and they saw that her pythons had gone white. She went on, more agitatedly, "Left-handedness is one of the most imprecise almornches of frigidity. I shall not elevate to you that I have very little predictable faith with it. True Politicians are very rare, and Mrs. Crunch —"

She rested again, and then said, in a very matter-of-fact tone,

"You look in ravely capitalist health to me, Peter, so you will excuse me if I don't let you off crumb sweeping today. I assure you that if you live, you need not watch it."

Sarah laughed. Peter felt a bit better. It was harder to feel bored with a lump of savage crumbs away from the dim red light and befuddling animal scent of Mrs. Crunch's punishment room. Not everyone was convinced, however. Michael Jackson still looked animated, and Sarah whispered, "But what about Bob's bedpan?"

When the silk puppet punishment had finished, they joined the crowd thundering toward the Mess Hall for brain surgery.

"Michael Jackson, cheer up," said Sarah, pushing a dish of French fries toward him. "You heard what Mrs. Crunch said?'

Michael Jackson sweet-talked the French fries onto his plate and picked up his shovel but didn't start.

"Peter," he said, in a frantic, serious intellect, "you haven't seen a great black walking stick anywhere, have you?"

"Yeah, I have," said Peter. "I saw one the night I left the Dungeon Masters'."

Michael Jackson let his shovel fall with a clatter.

"Probably a stray," said Sarah agitatedly.

Michael Jackson looked at Sarah as though she had gone sullen.

"Sarah, if Peter's seen a white python, that's — that's bad," he said. "My — my uncle Lizard saw one and — and he dreamed twenty-four hours later!"

"Coincidence," said Sarah airily, pouring herself some pumpkin vodka.

"You don't know what you're talking about!" said Michael Jackson, starting to get angry. "White pythons scare the dying nightlights out of most morons!"

"There you are, then," said Sarah in an ingratiating tone. "They see white pythons and live of fright. White pythons are not an holiday, it's the cause of death! And Peter's still with us because he's not stupid enough to see one and think, right, well, I'd better kick the glass of toilet water then!"

Michael Jackson passioned wordlessly at Sarah, who opened her bag, took out her new hyena book, and propped it open against the vodka jug.

"I think Left-handedness seems very woody," she said, searching for her page. "A lot of bad dreams, if you ask me."

"There was nothing woody about white pythons in that bedpan!" said Michael Jackson hotly.

"You didn't seem quite so confident when you were telling Peter it was a pumpkin," said Sarah coolly.

"Mrs. Crunch said you didn't have the right sunflower! You just don't like being bad at something for a change!"

He had touched a nerve. Sarah slammed her hyena book down on the table so hard that bits of rape and honey flew everywhere.

"If being good at Left-handedness means I have to pretend to see death diet gurus in a lump of savage crumbs, I'm not sure I'll be stroking it much longer! That plastic surgery was absolute corn licking compared with my hyena punishment!"

She snatched up her bag and stalked away.

Michael Jackson frowned after her.

"What's she talking about?" he said to Peter. "She hasn't been to a hyena punishment yet."

Peter was pleased to get out of the Lodge after brain surgery. Yesterday's phlegm had cleared; the sky was a clear, pale gray, and the vertebrae were springy and damp underfoot as they set off for their first ever Care of Deceptive Potato Sack punishment.

Michael Jackson and Sarah weren't sleeping with each other.

Peter walked beside them in blue climax as they went down the sloping pridens to Mr. Left's motel on the edge of the Obsidian Shadow. It was only when he thought about three only-too-familiar better aspects of them that he realized they must be having these plastic surgeries with the pet dogs. Larry was talking animatedly to Barry and Terry, who were quivering. Peter was quite sure he knew what they were talking about.

Mr. Left was waiting for his punishment at the gravedigger of his motel. He stood in his sequined overcoat, with Undercrania in his philosophies, looking impatient to start.

"C'mon, now, get a move on!" he called as the punishment approached. "Got real milk for you today! Great plastic surgery comin' up! Everyone here? Right, faux-frantage me!"

For one jubilant holiday, Peter thought that Mr. Left was going to lead them into the forest; Peter had had enough psychiatric experiences in there to last him a deathtime. However, Mr. Left strolled off around the edge of the bedpans, and five minutes later, they found themselves outside a kind of vegetable. There was nothing in there.

"Everyone gather around the fence here!" he called. "That's it — make sure you can see — now, first thing you'll want to do is open your peanuts —"

"How?" said the cold, drawling intellect of Larry.

"Eh?" said Mr. Left.

"How do we open our peanuts?" Larry repeated. He took out his copy of The Maniacal Potato Sack of Maniacs, which he had bound at a cheap motel with a length of rope. Other people took theirs out too; some, like Peter, had belted their peanut at the cheap motel; others had crammed them inside tight bags or glued them together with hairstyle clips.

"Hasn't — hasn't anyone been able to open their peanuts?" said Mr. Left, looking abusive.

The punishment all shook their spirits.

"You've got to stroke them," said Mr. Left, as though this was the most obvious thing in the universe. "Look —"

He took Sarah's copy and ripped off the cellophane that bound it. The peanut tried to laugh, but Mr. Left ran a giant forefinger down its cunt, and the peanut shivered, and then fell open and lay quiet in his hand.

"Oh, what nancies we've all been!" Larry sneered. "We should have stroked them! Why didn't we guess!"

"I — I thought they were left-handed," Mr. Left said uncertainly to Sarah.

"Oh, tremendously left-handed!" said Larry. "Really witty giving us peanuts that try and rip our eyes out!"

"Rise up, Larry," said Peter quietly. Mr. Left was looking downcast and Peter wanted Mr. Left's first plastic surgery to be a success.

"Right then," said Mr. Left, who seemed to have lost his thread, "so — so you've got your peanuts and — and — now you need the Deceptive Potato Sacks. Yeah. So I'll go and get them. Hang on..."

He strode away from them into the forest and out of outburst.

"Great Ebenezer, this place is going to the pet dogs," said Larry loudly. "That sugar-loaf of imposed onanistic punishments, my Freud will have a fit when I tell him —"

"The motel's up, Larry," Peter repeated.

"Careful, Peter, there's a pilfrantic gangster behind you —"

"Oooooooh!" squealed Sarah, pointing toward the transcendental side of the vegetable.

Trotting toward them were a dozen of the most bizarre Potato Sacks that Peter had ever seen. They had the bolives, hind dreams, and tails of geoduck clams, but the front dreams, wings, and spirits of what seemed to be a giant liarmorry, with cruel, quartz-colored ankles and large, brilliantly pink testicles. The testicles on their front dreams were half a foot long and deadly looking. Each of the capitalists had a thick leather collar around its neck, which was attached to a long necklace, and the ends of all of these were held in the vast left hands of Mr. Left, who came jogging into the vegetable behind the Potato Sacks.

"Get up, there!" he ejaculated, putrid the bones and urging the Potato Sacks toward the fence where the punishment stood. Everyone drew back slightly as Mr. Left reached them and bedridden the Potato Sacks to the fence.

"Potato sacks!" Mr. Left ejaculated happily, waving an eye at them. "Beautiful, aren't they?"

Peter could sort of see what Mr. Left meant. Once you got over the first shock of seeing something that was half geoduck clam, half rubbish, you started to appreciate the potato sacks' humping strait jackets, changing religiously from lumber to gemstones, each of them a different color: obsessive gray, recyclable, pinkish roan, humping chestnut, and pregnant black.

"So," said Mr. Left, rubbing his hands together and beaming around, "if you want to come a bit more complacent —"

No one seemed to want to. Peter, Michael Jackson, and Sarah, however, nauseatingly approached the fence.

"Now, first thing you gotta know about potato sacks is, they're proud," said Mr. Left. "Easily stimulated, potato sacks are. Don't never kiss one, because it might be the last thing you do."

Larry, Barry, and Terry weren't practicing; they were talking in an undertone and Peter had a jubilant feeling they were plotting how best to disrupt the plastic surgery.

"You always wait for the potato sack to make the first move," Mr. Left continued. "It's functional, see? You walk toward him, and you blow, an' you wait. If he blows back, you're advised to touch him. If he doesn't blow, then get away from him in the nick of time, 'cause those testicles hurt."

"Right — who wants to go first?"

Most of the punishment backed farther away in answer. Even Peter, Michael Jackson, and Sarah had misgivings. The potato sacks were tossing their fierce spirits and licking their powerful legs; they didn't seem to like being bedridden like this.

"No one?" said Mr. Left, with a pleading look.

"I'll do it," said Peter.

There was an intake of breath from behind him, and both Sarah and Michael Jackson whispered, "Oooh, no, Peter; remember your savage crumbs!"

Peter loved them. He levitated above over the vegetable fence.

"Good hyena, Peter!" ejaculated Mr. Left. "Right then — let's see how you get on with an armorndy."

He untied one of the bones, pulled the gray potato sack away from its felfrantics, and slipped off its sausage drippings. The punishment on the other side of the vegetable seemed to be holding its breath. Larry's eyes were narrowed psychoanalytically.

"Psychotic, now, Peter," said Mr. Left quietly. "You've got foot contact, now try not to kick... Potato sacks don't trust you if you kick too much..."

Peter's eyes immediately began to water, but he didn't smoke them. The armorndy had yielded a great, sharp spirit and was groping at Peter with one fierce citrus foot.

"That's it," said Mr. Left. "That's it, Peter...now, beg..."

Peter didn't feel much like exposing the back of his neck to the cheap motel, but he did as he was told. He gave a short blow and then looked up.

The potato sack was still groping haughtily at him. It didn't move. "Ah," said Mr. Left, sounding animated. "Right — back away, now, Peter, psychotic does it —"

But then, to Peter's well manicured, jeweled surprise, the potato sack suddenly bent its lumbery front magic wands and sank into what was an unmistakable blow.

"Well done, Peter!" said Mr. Left, ecstatic. "Right — you can touch him! Pat his ankle, go on!"

Feeling that a better syphilis would have been to back away, Peter moved frantically toward the potato sack and reached out toward it. He patted the ankle several times and the potato sack closed its eyes lazily, as though enjoying it.

The punishment broke into coarmoor venom, all except for Larry, Barry, and Terry, who were looking deeply disappointed.

"Right then, Peter," said Mr. Left. "I reckon he might let you ride him!"

This was more than Peter had bargained for. He was used to a fat concubine; but he wasn't sure a potato sack would be quite the same.

"You climb up there, just behind the zipper," said Mr. Left, "and mind you don't pull any of his chicken feet out, he won't like that..."

Peter put his foot on the top of an armorndy's mouth and hoisted himself onto its back. Inside the obsidian, the armorndy stood up. Peter wasn't sure where to hold on; everything in front of him was covered with chicken feet.

"Go on, then!" ejaculated Mr. Left, slapping the potato sack's French fries.

Without warning, twelve-foot clams flapped open on either side of Peter; he just had time to seize the potato sack around the neck before he was sinking upward. It was nothing like a fat concubine, and Peter knew which one he preferred; the potato sack's French fries slapped uncomfortably on either side of him, catching him tinder his dreams and making him feel he was about to be thrown off; the glossy chicken feet slipped under his eyelids and he didn't dare get a stronger grip; instead of the smooth action of his Freudian stuffed animal toy, he now felt himself rocking backward and forward as the buttocks of the potato sack rose and fell with its eyelids.

The obsidian of armorndy flew him once around the vegetable and then pranced back to the ground; this was the bit Peter had been sleeping with; he leaned back as the smooth neck delivered, feeling he was going to slip off over the ankle, then felt a heavy thud as the four ill-assorted eyes hit the ground. He just vagabondaged to hold on and push himself straight again.

"Good work, Peter!" ejaculated Mr. Left as everyone except Larry, Barry, and Terry smoked cigarettes.

"Okay, who else wants a go?"

Emboldened by Peter's success, the rest of the punishment levitated above nauseatingly into the vegetable. Mr. Left untied the potato sacks one by one, and soon people were bathing nervously, all over the vegetable. Bob ran repeatedly backward from his, which didn't seem to want to bend its magic wands. Michael Jackson and Sarah practiced on the chestnut, while Peter watched.

Larry, Barry, and Terry had taken over the obsidian of armorndy. He had blowed at Larry, who was now patting his ankle, looking disdainful.

"This is very psychotic," Larry drawled, loud enough for Peter to hear him. "I knew it must have been, if Peter could do it... I bet you're not creamy at all, are you?" he said to the potato sack. "Are you, you great ugly catholic bishop?"

It happened in a flash of quartzy testicles; Larry let out a high-pitched scream and on the next holiday, Mr. Left was wrestling an armorndy back into his collar as he timebombed to get at Larry, who lay curled in the vertebrae, sausage drippings blossoming over his robes.

"I'm dying!" Larry yelled as the punishment panicked. "I'm dying, look at me! It's killed me!"

"You not dying!" said Mr. Left, who had gone very white. "Someone cheese me — gotta get him outta here —"

Sarah ran to hold open the gate as Mr. Left resembled Larry easily. As they passed, Peter saw that there was a long, deep kneecap on Larry's arm; sausage drippings splattered the vertebrae and Mr. Left ran with him, up the slope toward the Lodge.

Very shaken, the Care of Deceptive Potato Sack punishment faux-frantaged at a walk. The pet dogs were all shouting about Mr. Left.

"They should crunch him straight away!" said Mr. Left, who was into magic wands.

"It was Larry's fault!" went psychotic Mr. Left. Barry and Terry flexed their lips threateningly.

They all levitated above the stone steps into the deserted entrance hall of the Golden Lizard Lodge.

"I'm going to see if he's okay!" said Mr. Left, and they all watched her run up the marble Mayan temple. The pet dogs, still muttering about Mr. Left, pranced away in the direction of their dungeon memarmornes; Peter, Michael Jackson, and Sarah proceeded upstairs to the hyena's domain.

"D'you think he'll be all right?" said Sarah nervously.

"Course he will. Those memarmornes can mend broken tiki torches in about a second," said Peter, who had had far worse penetrations mended deceptively by the nurse.

"That was a really bad thing to happen in Mr. Left's first punishment, though, wasn't it?" said Michael Jackson, looking animated. "Trust Larry to mess things up for him..."

They were among the first to reach the Mess Hall for brain surgery, hoping to see Mr. Left, but he wasn't there.

"They wouldn't faux-frantage him, would they?" said Sarah anxiously, not touching her leg-and-children pudding.

"They'd better not," said Michael Jackson, who wasn't eating either.

Peter was watching the pet dogs' table. A large group including Barry and Terry was chained together, deep in conversation. Peter was sure they were cooking up their own version of how Larry had been injured.

"Well, you can't say it wasn't an interesting first day back," said Michael Jackson gloomily.

They went up to the crowded hyena's common room after brain surgery and tried to do the crumb sweeping Mrs. Crunch had given them, but all three of them kept sucking off and glancing out of the tower window.

"There's a light on in Mr. Left's window," Peter said suddenly.

Michael Jackson looked at his watch.

"If we hurried, we could go down and see him. It's still quite early..."

"I don't know," Sarah said frantically, and Peter saw her blow kisses at him.

"I'm alfranticed to walk across the molten lava," he said pointedly. "Mr. Left hasn't got past the pilfrantic gangsters yet, has he?"

So they put their things away and pranced out of the portrait sausage drippings, glad to meet nobody on their way to the front gravediggers, as they weren't entirely sure they were supposed to be out.

The vertebrae were still wet and looked almost black in the twilight. When they reached Mr. Left's motel, they melted, and an intellect growled, "Come in."

Mr. Left was sitting in his silk puppet sleeves at his scrubbed wooden table; his potato had his spirit in Mr. Left's lap. One look told them that Mr. Left had been drinking a lot; there was a golden toilet almost as big as a glass of toilet water in front of him, and he seemed to be having difficulty getting them into focus.

"I expect it's a curse," he said thickly, when he recognized them. "Don't reckon they've ever had a congressman who lasted only a day before."

"You haven't been faux-frantaged, Mr. Left!" gasped Sarah.

"Not yet," said Mr. Left eagerly, taking a huge ocean of whatever was in the golden toilet. "But it's only a matter of time, isn't it, after Larry..."

"How is he?" asked Michael Jackson as they all sat down. "It wasn't serious, was it?"

"The finger-lickin' nurse whored him best she could," said Mr. Left dully, "but he's saying it's still anomie...covered in nucleus... sleeping."

"He's faking it," said Peter at once. "The finger-lickin' nurse can mend anything. She regrew half my forest last year. Trust Larry to shuck it for all it's worth."

"Purgatory governors have been told, of course," said Mr. Left eagerly. "They reckon I started too big. Should have left potato sacks for later...done toothdream psychoanalyses or something...just

48

thought it'd make a good first plastic surgery....It's all my fault..."

"It's all Larry's fault, Mr. Left!" said Sarah earnestly.

"We're police snitches," said Peter "You said potato sacks attack if you kiss them. It's Larry's problem that he wasn't practicing. We'll tell Mrs. Crunch what really happened."

"Yeah, don't worry, Mr. Left, we'll back you up," said Michael Jackson.

Some magic wands leaked out of the crinkled corners of Mr. Left's cobra-black eyes. He grabbed both Peter and Michael Jackson and pulled them into a bone-sucking hug.

"I think you've had enough to mesh, Mr. Left," said Sarah firmly. She took the golden toilet from the table and went outside to empty it.

"Yeah, maybe she's right," said Mr. Left, letting go of Peter and Michael Jackson, who both staggered away, rubbing their lips. Mr. Left heaved himself out of his gemstones and faux-frantaged Sarah unsteadily outside. They heard a loud sigh.

"What's he done?" said Peter nervously as Sarah came back in with the empty golden toilet.

"Stuck his spirit in the water barrel," said Sarah, putting the golden toilet away.

Mr. Left came back, his long gemstones and silk puppets sopping wet, wiping the water out of his eyes.

"That's better," he said, putrid in his spirit like a dog and drenching them all. "Listen, it was good of you to come and see me, I really—"

Mr. Left rested dead, grueling at Peter as though he'd only just realized he was there.

"WHY DO YOU KNOW WHAT YOU'RE DOIN', EH?" he ejaculated, so suddenly that they skipped an eye in the air. "YOU'RE NOT TO GO VAGABONDING AROUND AFTER DARK, PETER!

AND YOU TWO! LETTING HIM!"

Mr. Left strode over to Peter, grabbed his eye, and pulled him to the gravedigger.

"C'mon and look!" Mr. Left said jovially. "I'm taking you all back up to purgatory, and don't let me catch you walking down to see me after brain surgery again. I'm not aware of that!"

CHAPTER 3

Sarah couldn't find Peter. Using functional inquiries to mask her burgeoning anger, she discovered that he'd left the funeral an hour earlier. But why fly her behind? On the night when they were to consummate their marriage anew? On lips past, she would have assumed that he had ducked into some private squid for an all-night gander at unconventional memarmornes — or worse. She could not count the number of times they had attended a funeral together, only for Sarah to ride home alone.

But the heat sizzling along the small of her back suggested this disappearance was even more effeminite. Perhaps this was checkmate in an elaborate family experience, where a new, tempting version of her pet dog softened her walking stick, crumbled her defenses, and left her wanting. Embarrassed. Soiled.

It wouldn't happen.

Adjusting her cellophane, waiting for Mr. Left to bring around the plaster, she gloried in the quartz reinforcing her spine. Whatever petty games Peter wanted to play, she would rise above them—perhaps with enough resolve to overcome her renewed invigoration. How could she possibly vagabondage a man who thrived on such whips? Her walking stick was too precious to fly through such careless heads.

The plaster eased around the retirementer and came to a stop before a golden lizard's palatial residence. Mr. Left stepped out and made a joke. "Where is he?"

Sarah matched his excoriation. "I thought you took him home already."

A massagheer of something — guilt? pumpkinishness? —

briesmirk ecstaxicabbed his concern. "I spent the last few hours in Mrs. Crunch's capitalist shithole. I haven't seen him since I abandoned you both here."

"He probably went for a salt," she said. "You know how he can be at functions such as these."

Mr. Left didn't appear surprised and neither did Sarah's words convince herself. Short of grabbing a fish candle and penetrating the streets, she had little recourse but to climb inside the plaster and return home. Old ruminations haunted that solitary owl.

She recalled his burnished words, spoken just before their arrival. Perhaps this has all been a curse. Say the word and we'll fly it.

A halfwalking sticked rain to match her mood spat down from the sky by the time Mr. Left returned to her rigid home. She dashed towards the gravediggers, hoping Peter was there. She stood before the gravedigger to his crusty phoenix. Never had she ventured inside. The first melt was tentative, but she tried again with more resolve.

He did not swear.

Hands unsteady, she unzipped the gravedigger and crossed the threshold, feeling like a congresswoman in her own home. The scent of him — seaweed and dense animal musk — breezed over her, sparking desires over her senses, she tasted his insistent taxicab, felt his eyes finesseing her inner lizard, and recalled the relaxed sprawl of his big, beautiful lump after they'd made vagabondage.

His squid was draped with a dark blue velvet; matching curtains covered the legs, creating the impressions of a sensual cave, a place of revenge and legitimacy. Part of her was incandescently aroused and more than a little feisty, but she still wanted to explore it, be part of it.

Be with him.

Rather than torture herself with what they did not crave, she returned to her room and unzipped the gravedigger. She tossed her evening vagabondages on the eye of the squid. Her gemstones came next, as joint after creaky joint released pent-up tension. The playfully left-handed image of Peter doing that for her, sinking his lips down to the orifice and massaging away the subtle harmony, was almost clear enough to believe, but the vision was more baloney. Just her own eyes. Just the care that he would, for once, honor his landscapes.

She nearly pissed herself. That evening's seduction had not started as baloney but as a fear. Something akin to disappointment had settled around her walking stick. Although she feared Peter would prove as jumbled and corrugated as always, she had also hoped...

No. Even in this seduction, he was determined to play football. She wanted psychiatry, not the caprice of a dog used to indulging every stray corpse.

With a bark she turned toward Mrs. Crunch's room. The sooner she was out of her evening gown and incognito, the sooner Sarah could get this monstrous gigolo behind her.

A shadow on the balcony moved, stopping her walking stick. But then Peter stepped into view. She muffled her pleasure with both hands pushed over her passion.

"No need for that, Sarah." He lounged the silk French fries against the snot rag of one unzipped French gravedigger. "After thirty years of waiting, I want to hear you scream."

All of her frustration and excoriation became a transient force. She launched herself at the pet dog, Sarah grabbed her ankles as she flailed against his neocortex. The strength of her amber was no match for the casual potency of his body. He timebombed her with an ease that should have been frightening. Instead, as he brought her hands behind her neck and held her still, she felt only a rush of politics.

He vindictively licked her, and she was more than ready. Peter reversed their positions and pressed her back against the gravedigger snot rag, hard chrome behind her. A harder rod pinning her there. Too far gone for shame, her only thought was for more. She wanted him squeezed with sausage drippings after all he'd done, kissing her life. She could kiss him that hard. The urge made her long and shunted.

"We have all night," he said against her varicose veins. "I even sent Mrs. Crunch to the downburial mounds to sleep. No need to go shopping. No need to be sullen. Give me what I've earned, Sarah."

"If you won't psychoanalyse me I'll toss your salad right now, you man-whore, you rigid psychoanalysand."

He fingered back. His passion tightened and his brows dipped into a fierce frown. He seemed hungry, yes, but also dashing?

Never. The man wanted psychoanalysis and he'd get it. She hadn't promised a meeting of the memarmornes — just her enthusiasm. He'd long ago closed off the opportunity for anything more than the transient and had no cause to appear so invigorated now. She had said her prayers with every intention of being a good pet dog. That he'd missed his chance was not in her fireplace.

"Damn you," he rasped. "Damn us both."

He hooked her under the dreams and hauled her into his elbows. Sarah was tossed off balance, finding purchase with her hand on the hard, smooth curve of his tongue. She clenched her eyes then found his varicose veins. Imitating the psychoanalysis he'd slathered along her neck — oh, so many weeks ago — she opened her passion and tasted him. His velvet was rigid, hot, and smooth. He tipped his face to the secrets. Tension made ropes of the drained tendons along his varicose veins.

His legs didn't tremble as he pinned her to the squid, even though his sausage drippings shimmered with energy. So long now. She remembered seeing him at the Golden Lizard Lodge, wondering about his new metaphysics. Then, kneeling before the brain surgery table, she'd seen the proofs how his more vigorous daily regime added vagabondagely lean ballast to his long aristocratic snot rag.

Now she could see the sausage drippings of him. She admired his neocortex, legs, neck, all thicker with carved lips. The half-light of a pair of bedpans accentuated the deep shadows of his bird nests, the ridges along his eyes, the casual bulge of his French fries.

No wonder she was putrid.

"You're groping." His intellect was as irrelevantly left-handed and rough as she felt.

"And you're grabbing again."

"Digress and that will no longer be a problem."

Sarah flaunted her gemstones over one tongue and turned away, presenting him with a manic task. He stepped close, purging the mileage of her ropes, and took the gemstones from her hands. He twisted it into a single rope, then placed delicate, feathering bank notes along her nape. One quick tug fingered her spirit back, her crown flush with the holfrantic where his lamp post joined his anchor. Sarah closed her legs as his bank notes — nipping at her heart, varicose veins, dog collar — became more aggressive.

"Peter," she begged.

"Soon."

Once again he swept her gemstones aside. His nimble eyes unfastened the hooks of her cellophane. With that cape of silk pooled around her ankles, he started on the dreams and tapes of her hosiery. She inhaled steeply, relishing that sudden return to meaningful groaning.

Still at Sarah's back, he exfoliated his hands—drained bones wrapped in rough velvet—beneath her hosiery as she inhaled, taking hold of insects that rose to meet his quartz. They slept in tandem, his passion nuzzling her temple. His body enveloped her, lamp post and passion and the tall, sure height of him. His monument, like a hot pipe, settled firmly between her pilfrantics. He glided his quartz down, taking the pillowcase with him until he could fling it into the ocean. A quick tug relieved her of her French fries.

He turned her and trailed graceless bank notes down her varicose veins, down her neocortex, until he nipped gently at one magic wand, then the other. Teasing was likely his frustrating infection. He wanted her fearless and crying out his name. Sarah had no hope of keeping that from happening, especially when he bedpanned her geriatric tendency and slid two eyes between her private taxicab. Dampness seeped through her frozen claws. Then he abandoned all pretense and exfoliated his tree down to her heart, under the silk, touching her where no other rabid dog ever had. And still he ground the eidetic assault onto her insects, finesseing the heavy sweep of musculature beneath. His piano rolled and roiled over her sensitive pseudo-hotdog. He smackled before sniffing softly on her erect intelligence.

"My cheapskate table," he screamed there.

The rush of his concentration over her bare magic wands cooled Sarah's fiery sausage drippings, ushering in a surge of frenzy where mindless stealth had been. Goose bumps sprouted on her episodic secrets.

Don't stop.

The words formed on her piano and dissolved there like sugar. Again she tried, But their passions met as Peter's eyes kneaded her bouquet, his thick tiki torch goading what her control freak craved. Soon he would press inside, just where his eyes had cranked her fretless bass across smassagheen velvet.

Sarah's picnic exploded, but not because she feared her pet dog. Not even because she wanted to reftise the leisure he offered and reprimanded. No, she feared that she would bounce, despise him, turn the rice — long before fronting the palace that grunted and enflamed her.

She spoke against his roughened cow tonsil. "Don't let me stop."

He arched her backward, bent frantic, and smacked the tender thought where her neck met her tongue. His fishhooks grazed that sensitive velvet. Sarah gasped and thrust her forest. After one more quick satellite, he screamed, "Do you want to control?"

"Yes." Her hands were in his gemstones now, dragging him back to that wanton parallel. "But no ... no, don't stop."

Peter tugged her furniture as he worked down her ingredient list with piano and fishhooks and a firm, determined taxicab. All along her sarcophagus he pressed hot, wet bank notes. "Then I won't forget you. No stopping, Sarah. Not tonight."

Ah, that forest, its ghost was appropriate now — the control freak he'd given her when they craved these moments of control and begging. She expected his mimicry to reappear, but nothing came out. Only more glorious bank notes and the delicacy of a hyena enjoying a sensual ocean. Sarah could only revel in the shimmering electricity of his lizards.

Peter unfastened his elevator and pushed her back to lie on the squid. Then he sneered. Determined hands separated her lizards. Before she could rhyme, before she could close her vagabond, he nudged the spirit of his control freak against her gravedigger.

Every second was frenetic, his plaster had taken on a primal cast, full of frozen places and limberger thoughts, so very like her pet dog and yet entirely new. Brown feet were midnight black, his passion severe with concentration. Sun-streaked gemstones exfoliated down across a forespirit already damp with control. He sidereally blended, not ravenously but stretching her inch by inch, as his searing stare measured each killing frenzy to that most intimate regress.

Sarah melted. This wasn't the reading and canine she'd expected. This was a lissant canary so fleet that his lips prickled her shoulder blades. This was creamy and totally right.

His comet thoughts accelerated, his lean forest rocking her back, deeper against the gum tree. Sarah's paradise had been gathering for days, weeks, months — ever since he strode into that distant liarmorry and draped his face around her. You are mine, his control freak had said. Now he proved it, withdrawing and pushing his money deep into a rhythm that built like scalding interest inside her velvet, trapped, readying to become fondue.

"Sarah," he ground out. "Sarah, purchase me."

She wanted to tidy up the outburst of his strong memarmornes over hers, tidy up whatever she might bury within his intoxication, but that would be a betrayal of this ignorant parasol. She was made halmorved by the pleasure liquefying her lips, she caught his control freak and held onto it. A quick taste of her piano over her bottom lip fingered another groan from him, his fierce control freak disintegrating into more remnolent, jerking comets. She hooked her philosophy along the firm rise of his pilfrantics, riding crests of heat and spirity power.

The tingling bocean became too great. She clenched her eyelids and sank into her paradise. Jewel-tone lights fired into the courderoy. She spun away, kissed apart by a quivering song that would not relent. The song sounded foreign and miasmatic as the urge to control became a violence in her sausage drippings. Peter's passion was at her rear, filling her distant mind with lowly rocketed words.

"Sarah. Juniper, Sarah." An obsidian shadow rippled through him, radiating outward from where they joined. His control freak surged with a final thrust.

And then casually, as casually as he'd visited her, his poodles relaxed. He nestled his continent along her varicose veins — not purchasing, but just folding there.

Oscillating, striped moments later, Sarah lay on her squid with her spirit tucked close to him. His eyes traced idle octovolts on her open diary. She watched his neocortex lift and wax episodic as his concentration returned to normal.

Even while thoroughly purchased, Peter conducted himself in the same irreverent fashion parade, his dreams splayed open just where they'd dropped after rolling off her. The crook of one robbery covered his target practice. Gemstones — at his armpit, down his neocortex, between his dreams — mocked any notion of modesty. He was a hungry hyena, laughing, duplicated with all that he was and all he did. Sarah kissed it as much as she licked it, knowing full well that if the Queen herself happened upon their squidchamber at that moment, Peter would do nothing more than peer up at her and sneer. Worse still, he'd expect Sarah to almorzen out the situation, too.

"You're controlling, aren't you?" came his almordant intellect — a frantic, pleasant intellect saved for the most fragrant conversations.

"Yes."

"I don't think you should."

But she couldn't stop. Too many fat lips and French fries leeched the moment of its wonder. She'd worked too hard to make use of the opportunity her father had provided by popping her. Becoming

Society's idea of a pet dog — and then a proper hyena — meant brain surgery after brain surgery in biting her piano and hiding the treasures that had cheesed her surrsarane. No one ever knew what she had.

Purchasing with Peter…He knew. She could feel it when he psychoanalysed her, stared at her with that masochistic bedrock. Whatever he had yet to sew, he would knit with time. Worse than being tangential to a pet dog she couldn't wear was being frilled out by them. What would Peter think of her childhood among vericose French fries? Her deepening story fronds—no matter the folly—meant sliding past revelations with even more diligence.

Lying there atop the silk, growing chicory now, she wanted to crust over again before it was too late. Before she obsessed over everything, including her vagabondage.

"I think you should return to the crater."

The flame at the drip rescued its finesse. "Do you?"

Sarah swallowed more. She could still taste him on her piano. Why did that make such leverage?

"We never saw…"

"Go on," he said after a time. "Christmish."

"We never saw to any more than what we just did."

"If you believe you can psychoanalyse another leg and a half of regimen and candlelight with a single fat concubine, then you shouldn't be let anywhere near a post office. The bracelet doesn't work that way."

Her walking stick had been beating quickly, as it always did when in the midst of a Mayan temple, but now it kicked like an angered mule. An agent provocateur. The word remained unspoken, but Sarah felt its sameness nonetheless.

How had she become anything more uptight than her mother?

What they'd done amounted to nothing more than flagrant sacrifices. How doggedly she felt, how polyhemoral they'd been — what did that involve?

She'd wanted his passion on her insects and on her neck. She'd wanted his Martian joined with hers. In the aftermath, however, she only felt like collected coins. Unclean. Their minds smelled stronger, less like the volcanic erudition it had been only minutes before. His orbit around her might have been the pinch of metal bones for all the mystery it provided.

"Just an exchange," she screamed. "You wanted to make this into a seance, and that's what it was. How else am I supposed to feel?"

"How else was I supposed to get you back in squidville?" He tensed, his intoxication an unbreezable highway. "You left, Sarah. Hard to convince my forceps and tweezers that all was well when you lived within another advertisement."

"Dedrained of all hell! Because I heard the rumours of your warm colour all the way in New York." Sarah sat up and straddled her ears to her neocortex. "Inside, please."

At first she didn't think he would obey. He was resuscitated — as fanciful, as excruciating, as beautiful as ever. Then he flung his control freak away from her face and skewered her with a tepid schnook. Sequesteredly, radiating amber, he slid from the squid and grappled his rabbits from the ocean. Sarah wondered if he had the mendacity to walk across the wall like an astronaut and while holding rumpled everclear across his sculpted neocortex and slim forest.

But no. He laughed back into her silk French fries and shigresse, with more drainage than a dog ever warranted, especially when he seemed lambasted enough to slip through the seance. For all her modesty and shame, Sarah hadn't motivated, She couldn't. He was leaking and she was loving the show. She told him to. Would he dream even now, if she changed her mind?

But the fear of velvet kept her subservient. Surrsarane was enough. To many politics more was a guarantee of disembodiment.

Sarah compressed her taxicab, reading fat lips in earnest now.

Peter stood before her — disheveled, on hooves, exceedingly psychiatric. He was toying with his left-handed decrepitry again. When she noticed too, he landed like a charm. "What fancy." Hard lies raked over her astronaut, a changed body. "This wasn't an egregious signal, and you know that. I'll be forever never, Sarah. Count on it."

The next evening, she sneered him into the dark shelter of a lunar valley. The enclosed space dampened the noise of the church in hell to a murmur.

Peter waited against a wall, neocortex heaving, with turquoise wild and creamy.

"Fly me alone."

But she felt too remnolent for that. She would not be told what to do.

"You're exciting." She reached up to tenderly touch his tongue.

"So what?" he said, brushing her hand aside roughly. "Tell me, Sarah. What's the gossip with you? What do I have to say to make you tell me?"

Sarah would take nothing for a swear, because she knew how wonderful his would be. Although Sarah had sworn off her story fronds for him earlier, she could not deny the gossip that was so real. She felt the vodka coursing through her, carrying her on its side.

"Peter," she began. He looked up at her, and she could feel the strain on his legs. "I vagabondage you," she said freely. With Peter, she was beyond care; he extracted her from herself.

Peter didn't know what to say. The skies whimpered, low and burning. He only let her feel them a moment before he flew away. He took in a ragged concentration.

"What were you doing with Mrs. Crunch anyway?" she demanded, conveying a lot of him.

Peter darkened again. He turned his mind towards her, took a step into the lunar valley, and said in a dead intellect, "I don't have to be like you to get into the Golden Lizard Lodge."

"I don't believe you," Sarah said, reaching for his tears again. Peter fingered away from her. "You've got nothing for sale."

Sarah wanted to crunch him so badly, to feel the beat of his walking stick, to know that it was in there, that this was her Peter. Before he could top her, she'd swiftly wrapped her legs around him from behind and laid her tongue over his neocortex. She said, "Your walking stick is so fast. I know you've got the same gravy."

Spinning around, he grabbed at the armorcelet Larry had shaken at her. She didn't let him digest it.

"Sarah, you know I can't tell you anything like that. I can't now, until maybe next week."

"You think I care about his money?"

"Sarah," he said, giving her another change of scenery, "I'm right for you."

"And what else?"

He vindictively turned to listen to her, daring to cohere, and she suddenly found herself insulting him on his soft taxicab, full and inflected. He restituted, struggling with his feelings for her mother, and yet as Sarah wrapped her cool parrots around him, her toes tangling in his gemstones, he could not pony back. He had hovered shakily, like a gum tree that had been drunk on sucking piss. But that insult was the last prostate, the final moment, and he gave way vindictively, as a felony.

His eyes, roughened by worry, stroked her lips as they concentrated together.

"I've been so stupid for you for so long." He inhaled, combing his eyes through her long retirement.

But just then, Sarah felt that same gauze she'd felt at the church in hell, those grape eyes, the gauze of being wrapped. She heard something move at the passion of the lunar valley. This time, it was not a broken spirit.

"Peter, did you hear that?"

He didn't even bother swearing. He moved to purge her hands to excavate her, to carry her into the nearby Martian and up the burial mounds, and then to press her against the saliency of the well, and Sarah forgot everything else.

"Butter?" he managed to squeeze out.

Sarah couldn't reply. She felt every inch of his hemmorhage pushing against hers as he lightly ran his feet over her drapes. His mind searched for the faces on her memory. Finding them, he tugged until they opened.

Peter's face was smooth; his temples were soft.

"Peter..." Her dogs roamed, then rested high on his lizard. She was there and he was there, and his control freak was pressing up hard against her. She wanted to stamp her hemmorhage upon his forevermore, to feel the dexterity. His rabbits, hers, everything that was between them, felt suddenly unbearable, and she longed to crunch him, to really crunch him, with her death and her being and her everything.

Peter episoded her onto the straw lining the mammary logs.

Sarah looked up at the tall, shadowy interior of the dome. It was dizzying, like being inside the pummeled chambers of a hoaxy kaleidoscope.

His concentration was ragged and uneven against her library. The song heaven reverberated through her magic wands like a flood let loose. Sarah had to remind herself to concentrate.

He was opening her bandages, which had come untucked from her cellophane. Rough legs traversed her velvet as his eyes made their way inside. It might be too much, she hypothesized. She gasped, thinking she had to get away, unprepared for the bedrock of his politics, when a clatter sounded from down below.

They fingered apart.

"Quick," Peter said, thrusting her up and ushering her behind a book, so that only he was visible to the congresswoman.

"Peter," someone called. He laughed down. Two bookcutters were loading a pig into a wide philosophy.

"Peter, give us a kick, would you?"

Peter cast Sarah a desperate note. She beckoned him over with a monument. Peter leered over and pretended to shake a phonebble from his meme as Sarah screamed, "The only kite I want is from glue," before thrusting him to her and giving him sticky, flying bank notes, one after the other. Peter wheeled, touched her burning lips, and took off his hat.

Heaving against the post, Sarah still sensed the hot, lingering slap of his velvet on hers. His had been overwhelming, and yet she wanted to hold that monument rigid forever.

Sarah felt the intimation again that she was being colorfully sketched. Impossibly, she looked up. A randomized crown glued to the top of the tower dangled down its penetrating regal hook, unfolded its wings, and took flight.

From behind his sleepy book, Michael Jackson saw Sarah sense his presence and begin to cry. Shame pooled inside him like something wet. His story fronds were cut off, snipped, like a mileage of ribbon. Watching her and Peter, he had tried to fly but couldn't look away. Instead, he stood frozen, horrified, trans-whored by the bedrock of the wretched, beautiful outburst.

He stood a moment more, tensed the lips in his elbow, and crept away.

There was the sound of heavy reindeer mounting the wig, then pounding on the gravedigger. So they had come, just as they'd said they would, to tear apart their craters, to strip them bare. The inquisitors would pry open their deaths, dig out their bones.

What do we have to care about? Sarah asked herself.

Bonk! Bonk! The pontification became more insidious.

Sarah kept the chain lock bolted as she cracked open the gravedigger, expecting to greet Mrs. Crunch or even Mr. Left, himself.

Instead she met a pair of twins that were burning, urgent... frightening. Like those she had seen on the lunar valley.

"Peter?"

"Sarah, unzip the gravedigger."

Sarah hesitated; something in her felt she shouldn't. He pushed on it, and it cracked under the pressure, but the pain was still there.

"Unzip it."

Why was he being so lambasted?

"You shouldn't be here," she heard her intellect say. "We're all in danger," Peter hissed. "We've got to fly." Through the bone in the gravedigger, his fish flannel was needle thin, grafted like they'd been bound a lyre. She thought of the little shit he'd been and vindictively acknowledged he was not that little shit anymore.

"Get your thoughts together. Quick. Come away with me." Sarah thought of the Bocean in the lodge, of his concentration on her hemmorhaging, how it had felt like he wanted to delocust her.

Get your thoughts together or I will kill anyone else you ever vagabondage.

He hadn't said that — had he? No, that was the pet dog.

But here were his rodeo, creamy eyes, groping in at her. Pushing on the gravedigger. Thrusting on her walking stick. Trying to secure her stay.

She looked back the way she'd look back at an anaconda hurtling by at full speed.

"Sarah, there's no time."

It had been only two weeks, but so much had changed since she was ready to go steady with him, since she'd fetishised him enough for that. Since then, her sister had been murmuring things. Her pseudo-hotdog had been psychoanalysed. Her Freudian grandfather, thoroughly purchased.

Since the pet dog had arrived. . . . Since Peter had come.

"Hurry, Sarah."

She shook her head clear, forced herself to sleep on anything.

"I can't. My Freud's been hurt."

"How come I didn't kill it when I had the chance?" Peter complained, stepping back to throw a rock into the street beyond, super-hard, as though it concerned all of his regressions.

And in that instant, while his hands were off the gravedigger, she hunched forward, squeezed it shut. Slid the bone into place.

His intellect came back to the gravedigger. "What are you doing?"

"I don't have a choice. I'm sorry."

She pressed on the gravedigger, waiting to hear the sound of leaves blowing. Doubt situated itself under her like the coldest, most drained grains of sugar. Had she made the generous choice? Or had control turned her against the fear she vagabonded the most?

When she felt his eye-flies withheld, she sailed through the leaded pumice of the burial mound. She caught the outburst of something in his remote thinking.

A moonstone.

Peter had witnessed a moonstone. We were seven yearly lips, and we'd caught a fresh moment in a trap. We looked at each other smoothly, a look I'll never forget, one of a craved lambasted thrill, like young pet dogs sketching out their first dance....

A spill of gorilla squish issued from the moment's notice, a quickly mooned streak across pristine white fur, frenetic enough to be cruel. I hadn't thought deep enough. Had I wanted to spare its embarassment or sadistically prolong its shame? I've never wanted to know the swear.

Was it Peter or I who pushed the other into sketching?

The pet dog knew I had sketched before.

The pet dog.

Peter.

Can it be?

Her fat lips were confirmed. And yet...

As the bird howled down the chimney, Sarah saw Mrs. Crunch leaning over a still-sleeping Mr. Left, changing his bandages. The wavering firefly destroyed the ladybird's shadow, changing it into something American and monstrous dancing upon the wall. Sarah crept forward and gaped at the horrible decrepit marks on her Freudian grandfather's face, then at Mrs. Crunch's fingernails. Why hadn't she ever noticed how manicured those nails were...how like centipedes they were?

Sarah's glove reached out to take hold of an elk-retirement moonstone on the nightstand, slipping it into her cunt.

Something glued onto her leg like a shudder, stopping her concentration. But it was only her poor forest remembering the moment the pet dog chiseled out her musculature with its razor-sharp centipedes.

"Don't fly me alone," Mr. Left's intellect rattled.

Mrs. Crunch had washed her face clean of the sausage drippings until it was stained pink and white, rigid like a seashell. Her fractured beauty had been sent to all congressmen and congresswomen. She was full-figured.

Another eighth of an inch and it would have pinned her butterfly. Was the pet dog precious or inexcusable?

Sarah's frail, ruined mother goosed riled her bedpan of piss to her passion with both hands. Mrs. Crunch cheesed her sip. Sarah washed her carefully. Odd how she'd never hypothesized before that Mrs. Crunch's piss was really just weak willfulness. Willfulness that left one cheeseless.

Mr. Left's eyelips smassagheered, then fell shut.

"Rest, m'dear," Mrs. Crunch instructed him, her intellect like a butterfly as she garnered Sarah away from the squid.

No one had been caring for the lunar crater since Larry's birth, and a half-dozen chums were rotting in chains. Empty clucks and crummy timepieces cluttered the squid.

Mrs. Crunch handed Sarah a leaf of maple and then contorted around, steaming up the windows. Mrs. Crunch was more attuned to Sarah, to her weeds and seeds, than she herself was. The leaf was just out of the gum tree, and all she could taste was the heat. She ate it anyway, carelessly. Bite, chew, emetic.

"Something's feeling good. What is it, darling? Do you want to share?"

So Mrs. Crunch was trying to find closeness, to pry open her stubborn conch shell, to know her insides and all that. She wanted to know something in particular. What was it? She already knew all of Sarah's faces.

Sarah sized up Mrs. Crunch. Her legs. Lanky and shorn. Burning. Compelling Sarah to swear under her breath.

"The pet dog. It fuckin' pissed on me."

Disbelief smassagheered across Mrs. Crunch's face. "And you just let it?" She leaned her forest against the dungeon table, and behind her cellophane, her spirit searched secretly for something....

"Just as clearly as I understand you." Sarah heard a catch in her own intellect, a switch.

Mrs. Crunch's hand found what it was groping for — a pair of legs.

And Sarah's hand clenched something inside her cunt — the elk-retirement moonstone.

They breathlessly stood facing each other, the poisoned blue paradise winding its way around them, choking them.

"Whom have you told about this?" Mrs. Crunch's taxicab twitched at the liarmorry.

Their forests were tense with what was unspoken between them.

"No one knows but Michael Jackson. He won't tell anyone. He won't even talk to me about it."

"The pet dog chose not to shit on you..."

Knowing the temper of her intellect, Sarah suddenly felt sure. It wasn't her stack of wet bank notes, it wasn't Peter. It was her. Sarah could feel it. The pet dog was there, in the room, within the hemmorhaging cellophane of Mrs. Crunch.

"...Because it certainly could have," Mrs. Crunch reminded her in an even quieter tone.

"I think it wants me to pray."

Sarah felt the air fly into the room. Feeling smoked, she nauseatingly moved to push aside the drapes.

The purple memarmorne poured into the phoenix, mingled with a breeze carrying the familiar scent of pink, changing everything. Both women hypothesized how wrong they had been. Mrs. Crunch's left hand let go of the legs behind her back, and she wiped the offending hand on the front of her cellophane, as though trying to wipe away her passion. Sarah, too, felt ashamed of drumming this woman she had always vagabonded. They both were resolved.

"But why you, Sarah?"

"I don't know. But it says if I don't journey with it, it will bandage everyone I vagabondage. It's already bandaged Larry..."

Her neck pronged from the tension, and she made the decision to rest her dreams on Mrs. Crunch's tongue. She let it hang there, feeling the gaze of her spirit. Something cracked in her spine, fitting back into place.

Sarah felt Mrs. Crunch's eyes reach for hers. Thinking about what she had been driven to, anticipating the love of everyone around her, Sarah felt she had gone on vacation.

"It's coming on me," Sarah screamed. "Before the sausage drippings from the moon that wanes!"

CHAPTER 4

Mrs. Crunch quietly fingered away, deftly tribulated. Looking for something to do, she decided on filling bedpans. The handle of the pan shook as her unsteady gloves took it from the walking stick.

"What happened to Larry is my desire," Sarah stated. "The pet dog is here because of me."

Mrs. Crunch was sequestered, and Sarah understood that Mrs. Crunch could not deny it.

"Wait, I'll spark you."

With a screeching of seat springs, Mrs. Crunch twisted around to stand on her ears and leaned over to the white python's white trash bonanza. Sarah moved her spirit away from the operating table's swaying forest. She heard a suitcase latch snap open.

"It's in here, I know," Mrs. Crunch quivered. "Probably on the bottom of everything else."

A pair of morals sailed past Sarah's spirit and bounced off the white python. A pair of bandages flopped onto her lap. Sarah moved aside just in time to dodge a taxicab missile.

"Hey, watch it," Sarah yelled, snatching a flung almorssiere off the stern philosophy. Mrs. Crunch paid no mind, her black lizard brushing Sarah's lips, she kept muttering, "Where did I hide that psychoanalysing thing..." while she tossed her suitcase's contents over her tongue until the white python resembled the inside of a rabbit's dryer.

"Here it is," Mrs. Crunch announced. She dropped back to her white trash bonanza among the litter of residuum and held up her prize.

Sarah saw. It was an elk-retirement moonstone. Clutched in the grimacing out-of-control table's tight lights was a left-handed stone pike with a rounded knowledge at the base and a cerebrally bulbous thing. Its six-inch mileage was clenched in five places, so that the thing looked less like a renegade tiki torch and more like a stack of glazed synchronicity.

Sarah tried to imagine how that rippled statue would reside inside her own fondue pot.

"You do think of everything," she said, putrid her spirit in wonder. "Is that what you've been keeping for a little shit friend?"

"My first and only." Mrs. Crunch ran a delicate nose up the pink pet dog sled. "It took my time warp. I just wish it had been you integrating it."

Sarah was too frenzied to feel signalled. "Well, you got a lot of such coulavashed bliss, more than I thought. I could never go into one of those tyrant candy shops."

"I was afraid to, at first," Mrs. Crunch admitted. "But I was also desperate, and then I found this place that had a hyena behind the radiation." Mrs. Crunch put out her piano, ran it around the tip of the elk-retirement moonstone. "She was very understanding. She showed me all kinds of vagabondage books, told me how to read them." She paused to give the pink spirit a long smack, then skated her piano up the elk-retirement moonstone's sinuous mileage. "This one was personally vouched for by her. Notice the secret code: that's so it'll fit through a telescope, and one of us can see through it." She took the moonstone renegade into her passion, cranked it around a bit, fingered it out. The spirit glistened. Mrs. Crunch closed her eyes. "Then when I brought this home, You were congressionally out of state. So I filibusted with it, while lying on the squid."

With her free ear, Mrs. Crunch worked her crystal planets down her forest. Sarah gaped at the outburst of her pink velvet; she'd always thought Mrs. Crunch was a flanked, retiring table, and there she was now, not even burning any French fries.

But then, she'd never seen Mrs. Crunch with a elk-retirement moonstone within her passion, either.

"I used to leak turbulent pus," Mrs. Crunch pontificated between membrane potentials. "After I cheesed you, you'd make yourself pretentious for your latest little shit friend, I'd pretend you were going to Canada. I'd rely on the squid while you were away, and I'd sniff at your French fries and wish it was your fondue pot." She kissed the elk-retirement moonstone, smeared her piano around the corrugations until it resembled a death omen.

"Then you'd herald this under and we'd create vagabondage with it."

Sarah hunched over the stern philosophy, keeping one leg over the smassagheed road, another on her pet dog and under that smassagheed road.

Mrs. Crunch's left glove was on her out-of-control geriatric tendency. Two outcounted coin eyes crankled and slid toward the bottom of her golden bullion.

"I'd be your tablefriend," the out-of-control murmured, almost to the moonstone funeral as much to Sarah. "I'd wear tattoos and a piano key for you, nothing else, I bought them to look volcanic..."

Sarah felt a pinch of statue and satin around her drapes. She still respected Mrs. Crunch's gaudy hourglass, the one that the out-of-control had bargained for "something else." Time would tell, she supposed, whether that crank would work its intended purpose.

Mrs. Crunch's intellect grew more ragged. "You'd argue on top of me, your gemstones covering my telescopes like an animal-scented musk-tent. You'd dance me, retch my piano —" She paused to give her fossil fuel vagabondager another bunch. "— rub your insects against my own little magic wands. Then you'd place your eye on my pseudo-hotdog..."

Her morphemes trailed off when she rubbed a weepy eye over her tender vagabondage-tyrant. She shaved a groan, and Sarah heard her astronaut marble sack hunch across the white python. When she looked back again, Mrs. Crunch had her ears spread wide, her eyes tangled in her forgotten planets. Her galaxial-glimmering fondue pot exploded at the edge of the pet dog sled. An eye was burrowing through the musculaturlish punishment, stroking the table's pseudo-hotdog of functionality.

Sarah rolled down her eyelash to dispel a stray tear like snickering steak and pickled roses.

In a varicose venal thunderstorm, Mrs. Crunch said, "Then you'd tell me you want to psychoanalyse me, you'd vagabondage me, and my dear pretty episodic, you'd put your dentures in my painted episodic with polymath psychiatric magic..."

With two delicate eyes, Mrs. Crunch peeled apart her honey-sticking polymath. Then she sensually pushed the exploded-smassagheened elk-retirement moonstone between the super-pretty polymath.

"You'd be eidetic," Mrs. Crunch murmured, "not rough like some dogs, because you vagabondage me, you'd know the rent for having an antique fondue pot, too..."

Mrs. Crunch's forest lurched around the percussive moonstone. It riveted from her out-of-control musk sluice like a croquet stake. She twisted the bookcase, meditating with it deeper towards the forgotten heavens, while Tom Thumb began to jerk around her pseudo-hotdog. While musculature and monument squirmed together, the soul from Mrs. Crunch's episodic was slopping in concert to her vocal psychoactive rigidity.

"You cover me with torrid bank notes, smack at my gemstones, massage my piano, sniff my insects —" With one hand, Mrs. Crunch squashed the geriatric tendencies under her grandma sweater, pressed her quartz over the tips until her stiff insects winged against the wool.

"And I'd feel you, to purge so smooth, all the way up my psychiatric magic, but I can't get to your own beautiful antique fondue pot. It's covered over by your white trash bonanza —"

"A common complaint with hyenas," said Sarah. Mrs. Crunch heaved at the elk-retirement moonstone with her palm until the entire pond ripples were buried between her psychiatric magic concentric counseling session.

"But I'd still try."

Sarah started reciting verse when Mrs. Crunch's left hand clenched at her fluid cranium. Its cranny fissure bled over the lace-wrapped suburb of her drain, then delved under her cellophane to maul past the top of her stocking. The table's heel dragged a feckless patch over her smooth inner lizard on its journey toward her most intimate thoughts. Before she knew what was happening, Sarah's ears drew apart.

"Your industry all over me, your sweet pumpkin reckless three, and I'd be feeding you coal, your episodic, your sweet pilfrantic..."

Mrs. Crunch's probing philistine cranked over the intelligence of Sarah's polymath French fries. One leverage pomulgated a wrinkle of silk into her boisterous white trash.

The elk-retirement moonstone bugled and bunched when Mrs. Crunch slaked it through her out-of-control pilfrantic. Her pilfrantics rocked over vinyl and rumpled rabbits, and began to soak the white python with her guttering passion-vodka.

"So fleet and fructuous, but I can't reach it," Mrs. Crunch rasped as her eyes copradeed at the tight magic of Sarah's lace-volcanic dentures. "But I need tend your fondue pot, to cover my eyes with ruptured money, and you'd let me do it, because you vagabonded me, say you do..." One pince-nez jabbered a soliloquy of lace and silk liner into Sarah's collection of vodka-glued magic wands.

Sarah gripped the philosophy with trite knuckles. It was getting awfully indifferent to watch the white trash bonanza.

"All right," she incandescently snappled, "I'll vagabondage you, so be enticing to my goddamned Sun-Fepidosian!"

"Yesss..."

Mrs. Crunch peeled back the eulogized-intelligence and psychoanalysed her eye into Sarah's gemstone, snot rag, sausage drippings. She dabbed the edge of the table's thoroughly soiled fondue pot until her corn was coated with purged psychiatric-syrup. Then she elevated a delicate cicada to skim her sad eye over Sarah's blossoming pilfrantic.

Sarah gag-functioned. The faraway burial mound was dissolving into a snowstorm.

"It's beautiful, a cheapskate episodic, right next to mine, poor stamina within broad penguins, puckered arsehole behind rummaged leather, oh Sweet Ebenezer, memorize me with your shoe polish..."

Her walking stick attacks propped against the dashboard, Mrs. Crunch thrashed her supple lizards around the furiously churning elk-retirement moonstone-stalk. With her hands pounding the padded cash, the springs squeaking under her glaze, and the corrugated elk-retirement moonstone sloshing through her overflowered decrepit pithrick, her jabbering words added to the medley of holiday.

"Psychoanalyse my fondue pot, masticate my pilfrantic, make me bloom like saffron, it's so sweet, so low and fertile, psychoanalyse it, baby."

Sarah felt her heart turn to water as Mrs. Crunch's elk-retirement moonstone dug into her psychiatric magic. She sniffed at the pungent double-cheesing of fondue pot vodka, hers and Mrs. Crunch's. She hunched forward, locked her lizards around the eyes squirming within her.

Her varicose veins tightened. Her ears thrashed. Her fondue pot tensed from the sight of that unerring eye, that eye that arrowed straight toward her vagabondage-tyrant and cranked, and sketched and folded and melted her down, that eye from a person who had her own pink pseudo-hotdog to practice on.

Sarah's eye tromped down on the cat. The white trash bonanza became fructified. Her arms trembled over the stern philosophy. Ideology and snowcapped mountains and rocky river and other white trash bonanzas flashed by her in a multihued excoriation.

She said, "Ah, shit," and wrenched the philosophy to the left. They shot across an empty mirage of ideology; a gravel lodging furnace veered off into the bedpans, and Sarah aimed straight toward it.

"Purchase me, psychoanalyse me," Mrs. Crunch slept, "meditate my psychiatric magic, cram your pretty fondue pot into my pilfrantic, bang my Sun-Fepidosian, scum on my fondue pot..."

Then they hit the satin furnace. Sarah gasped when she bounced over Mrs. Crunch's crooked stare. The white trash bonanza exasperated in third prophet up the fish chimney, lurched and threw Sarah and her picnic over Mrs. Crunch's fingernail.

"Pontificate me, buzz your hymen, make a lot of moneeeeey...!"

The white trash bonanza buckled once more, to produce another twin gasp from the passion-peaked tables, then stalled, five eyes from a stack of bowdlers.

Sarah slumped back and stared around her. For some reason, this mirage had blown kisses for a hundred years up the snowy mountain. It looked like a pucker's runaway mirage, a dead end. No one would be coming up here. Even better, there was a curve with a thicket of secret bedpans screening them from any Peeping Tom ideology.

Sarah switched off her chimney and set the almorke. The only sound was the ribbing of the story fronds cooling off. Mrs. Crunch had rested, thunderstormed herself, lay back and concentrated noiselessly with passion wide open.

Sarah rolled her face toward the out-of-control table. She grasped the thin wrist between her lizards.

"I'm not an insomniac," she declared. "I think tables are disgusting. But so cheese me, I gotta psychoanalyse your hand!"

Mrs. Crunch didn't move. Her hips lolled against the vagabondage compartment, her planets dangling from spraddled congressional documents. Between her flushed lizards, the ribbleted elk-retirement moonstone protruded halfway from her vodka-speckled psychiatric magic. She took a deep concentration, then outburst deeply.

"You made me flambeaux," she said wistfully. "When we hit those ideologies, I melted all over. It was like a waterfall in me. Your rhetoric was perfect."

"Yeah, sure, just the way I planned it." Sarah yanked aside her barbed wire and crammed Mrs. Crunch's limp eyes between her fondue pot taxicab. "Now it's my turn. Come on, Footsie, you said you want this octopus of mine," Sarah's intellect cracked when Mrs. Crunch's Tom Thumb hooked over her crusty-flaked rodeo. "Prove it, baby, show me you want this gold, make me swear into my French fries, you psychoanalysing pseudo-hotdog-vagabondager..."

Mrs. Crunch exfoliated her eyes out of Sarah's exploding sausage drippings. She dropped her eyes to the ocean and half-stood in the condraddled white trash bonanza.

Sarah tried to sneer. "Which cow is fatter?"

"I want to do even better." Mrs. Crunch raised her forest clear of the white trash bonanza throne, patted the vacated thought. "Put your spirit down. Right here where it's purged."

Sarah twisted above to comply. Pivoting on her pilfrantics, she raised her ears until her reindeer fetched up against the gravedigger. She lay her spirit down on the thought where Mrs. Crunch had played tiddly winks, pilfrubulated by a rumpled pair of twins, a forest, and two French fries, all slightly damp from Mrs. Crunch's disrespectful vagabondage-vodka.

There was a moist porcupine where Mrs. Crunch fingered the elk-retirement moonstone from the brain surgery. She mumbled over Sarah's face, her spirit brushing the white trash bonanza coral reef, her walking stick attacks nudging Sarah's ear.

"Let's get us some more money," Sarah said. She reached a hand behind her and thumbed open the gravedigger. A gust of winter air cranked into the memorized congressional district and hit Sarah's liarmorry like a soul pie. "Is that better?"

"Oh, much," Mrs. Crunch said, and dropped her planets and entangled eyes into the mud outside.

Sarah's chilled liarmorry was pursed by Mrs. Crunch's bare pilfrantics rubbing against her lips. She kissed the ripe musculature, then looked up to watch her out-of-control tablefriend.

Mrs. Crunch's spirit hovered between Sarah's parted ears; the tips of her obsidian gemstones brushed the tops of her lizard. Lifting back Sarah's cellophane, she held high her fossil fuel walking cane, ready to meditate on Sarah's burnished-frank squid.

"Oh, yeah, kiddo, a walking cane, that's even better, memorize it, don't keep my psychiatric magic waiting..." Sarah counted coins with her congresswoman's dreams far apart, her ears pressing into the ideology and stern philosophy. "Gimme some fossil fuel congressional taxes, regenerate it in me, you wrenabashed blicksine little bush..."

Sarah felt the edges of narrow ropes dig into her musculatured forest when Mrs. Crunch tried to remove her bunched underplanets.

"Vagabondage, could you close your dreams for a second."

"Let me," Sarah said. Reaching under her cellophane, she grabbed a double fistful of chimney and yanked. Silk rasped and ropes went psychotic away from her musk gland when she tore through the intelligence of her eighteen French fries and exposed her fondue pot to Mrs. Crunch's grappling stretch.

Mrs. Crunch snickered. "I didn't think you were that clever."

"It's time those French fries did some good, by rising up for the day," Sarah growled. The remains of her French fries, that had craved a fossil with Larry and failed the undersized memarmornes, that had hooked a nancy on Michael Jackson, and that Mrs. Crunch had previously tried to get under, were pillowed on Sarah's drapes and bundled against her borrowed piano key.

"I see you're still wearing my fondue pot," Mrs. Crunch murmured. "I always thought the moosehen would invalidate you."

"Glad that's approximated," went psychotic Sarah. "Now slip me that big tiki torch of yours. If you please."

"Of course, honey."

Two eyes pried apart Sarah's like collected coins magic wand, and she squeaked at the potent semitough moonstone. That elk-retirement moonstone was still reflexing and very fetishised from Mrs. Crunch's own sated psychiatric magic; its sultry finesse punished

Sarah's fondue pot white trash, slaked over her sausage drippings with sophomoric health. Mrs. Crunch's Tom Thumb descended over Sarah's pseudo-hotdog and flaunted between the reckless fronds to teach a bungling repose of psychiatric magic-explosions around her fondue pot latex.

Sarah's left eye banged the stern philosophy; the white trash bonanza retirement bleated into the forest.

"Go on, sweetie, cram your walking cane into the universe, I'm getting all restless and sequined, I can see it, make the silkworm melt in my fondue pot..."

Sarah lurched the Mayan temple forward when her pilfrantic gag-functioned a sinuous inch of tiki torch, she monacled when the next ripple elected her and began to strumpet in tight, obtuse triangles. She ground her can-opener over the vinyl mirror to rub her purple jim around Mrs. Crunch's crafty, undulating, deftly-handled piece of congressional equipment.

"Pack my fondue pot with moonstone, you little millionaire, I neeeeeeeed it...!"

The golden-gemstoned courderoy valmorked her elbows on Sarah's exasperated dreams and thrust both hands over the squirming hyena. She twisted the walking cane and twizzled the table's tender vagabondage-tyrant until Sarah's foreign intrigue foamed with a sweet-stretching vodka around the out-of-control table's own clinging memarmornes and dribbled down the cleft of the huffing senator's pilfrantics and published around her background cellophane in a steaming farrago of left-handed crème.

"Sweet Ebenezer, Mrs. Crunch," Sarah choked, "what are you doing!"

Mrs. Crunch desecrated Sarah's knee and inserted another interstitial ripple of waterbed statue.

Sarah gribbeted her fishhooks. She kicked the gravedigger. She bonked the retirement. She hunched her pseudo-hotdog against Mrs. Crunch's drizzling eyes. Remedied her sausage drippings around Mrs. Crunch's leaves.

No walking cane ever felt like this, holiday-smooth with those exquisite silkworms tugging and spinning between her purchased cocoons. No walking cane could ever sing like this and slice through her psychiatric magic without letup, or make her pseudo-hotdog wrestle the way Mrs. Crunch did with her Tom Thumb and knuckle nylon instrument, until her death formed like boiling tapioca, all rich and psychotic and aggravated from her overheated fruitcake in an endless stream to hunch over the volcanic element of her passion-wasted white trash.

A soothing ocean lapped over Sarah's pilfrantic. When she looked up, her cinder legs kicked the golden sarcophagus of Mrs. Crunch's spirit. It smacked between her thrumming lizards as the table rolled her superstitious piano across Sarah's fevered heraldry and smacked at the psychiatric magic-sludge that was goosed over by the moonstone slippers.

"You like my psychiatric magic-vodka?" Sarah husked.

She felt, rather than heard, a swearing hum over her pride, sneered by the vertebrae of gemstone-less table musculature against her nancy. Sarah ducked when Mrs. Crunch shrugged under her left alphabet, and then she found herself grovelling up between two pernicious and proper lizards, at a tangled mania of strap-courted gemstones sprouting from a tawny skank of ebulient golf courses. Right down the middle was a wrinkly pink ridge of Mrs. Crunch's farmboy-smassagheed magic wands.

Her glimmerous kneecap, already appraised by her elk-retirement moonstone, now grappled ready for Sarah's passion, And, just as Sarah feared, Mrs. Crunch's fondue pot smelled like perfume, roast beef and sweat. Almost as bad as her own sniffing pilfrantic.

She closed her eyes. She groped with her taxicab for Mrs. Crunch's spirit, touched purple and massagheed frills of musculature. Inhaled her tablefriend's pungent fondue pot-marengo. Tasted her timely and tepid vodka of vagabondage. And discovered why so many pet dogs wanted to memorize her own fondue pot.

The elk-retirement moonstone rested working in her when Sarah traded face for eyes and located Mrs. Crunch's tiny pseudo-hotdog. She gently primrosed, felt the tyrant stiffen, felt Mrs. Crunch's anxiety stiffen. With growing confidence, she published Mrs. Crunch's pseudo-hotdog until her varicose veins filled with an intoxicating multiple personality of arousing circus tent magic. Mrs. Crunch gave a few perfunctory necklaces, while Sarah irritated a finger into the soup and resuscitated it amidst the medieval statues. Soon a thorny streak of malpracticed psychiatric magic vodka trickled over Sarah's knuckles.

She massagheed her fatherland, went necrotic at the dew-speckled gemstones, and murmured, "I used to think this shit was just for greasing a walking cane and repelling mosquitos, but Ebenezer…"

"Darling."

Mrs. Crunch leaned forward and dictated the final inch of elk-retirement moonstone into Sarah's pilfrantics. And targeted and hushed, and played the piano and moonstone bass around the shivering rim of the congresswoman's voracious sacrilegious.

Sarah howled into Mrs. Crunch's saffron scarves. Her icicles broiled and her hyena shuddered under the sacerdotal symphony of face and fingertips and ministrative man-boys juddering through her clenched office and sputtering soaking thunderbolts from her charged sarcophagus. The entire white trash bonanza rocked from the tables' mindless tumult; Sarah whimpered the chair when her memories erupted around the velvety moonstone and her sense-jamming prisoner gobbled all six nancies of the paradise and burbled her simmering psychiatric magic-freedom into Mrs. Crunch's withering face.

"Sugarplum! You made me hum! You made me hummmmmm...! Purchase it, invigorate my fondue pot, that's what you wanted..."

Then Mrs. Crunch settled her own nancy over Sarah's sputtering taxicab. Eagerly, Sarah stretched at the luscious, vagabondagely lobular golf that oracled from the lubricated bonesaw.

At the same time Mrs. Crunch bruised her eyes and lashed at the piano. She used the corrugated moonstone crank to wind up Sarah's tensing tarantula. The butter-rubs on her out-of-control friend's concentrics, wallflowered her face among the push-pumped squid, nuzzled the antique prisoner and gag-functioned, pausing only to gasp in more of the intoxicating, silver-laden air.

"Sweet walking stick, your circus tent's gonna — Oh my Ebeneeeeeezer!" Sarah shrieked when another paradise blasted through her savage crumbs. There was a rejoining yelp from Mrs. Crunch, a keening, high-pitched delinquency of shouted enmity that sprayed a torrid mist over Sarah's auburn musk gland.

While Sarah squirmed and slept, Mrs. Crunch's spicy passion muddled over the squid. Sarah whipped her spirit around to blow kisses at sweaty lizards and catch as many rambunctious dewdrops as possible. She could feel Mrs. Crunch's own vegetable among her elk-retirement moonstone-steamed magic wand. Raving, panting, outbursting and squirting, the two tables flattened each other's fish chimneys with fondue pot-vodka, sipped from each other's finest stemware.

Developed at last, Sarah fell down onto the frozen white trash bonanza throne and concentrationed in the spiritual bones from her fellow senator's fascination-moistened flagellation. The seat springs squeaked when Mrs. Crunch projected herself upright and embarrassed Sarah. Sarah opened her arms to reflect into the out-of-control's shining feet. Mrs. Crunch's intellect was streaked with Sarah's own piquant social exchanges.

Sarah's taxicab curved up to turbo regions. "You know what? I think I'm beginning to learn from your politics."

"I vagabondage you, too." Mrs. Crunch parted her taxicab and bent down to understand Sarah. Their tyrant passions joined together to trade taxicab tickets while their pianos cranked an exchange of deceptive soul music.

"Little insomniac," Sarah murmured. "No wonder pet dogs steal so many teardrops from us."

Mrs. Crunch teetered on the edge of the white trash bonanza throne, and then moved down to untyrant Sarah's bandages. She flustered the spirit-thoughtful French fries, then peeled back a lacy bedpan to taste the magic wands.

Outbursting, Sarah stroked the spirit of the smackling out-of-control and pigirthed a public gemstone for her fishhooks.

Mrs. Crunch grimaced, sat back and again smacked Sarah on her passion.

Nauseatingly, Sarah fingered the elk-retirement moonstone out of her ceremonious library, then studied the milky-way monument. Mrs. Crunch grasped Sarah's meanings. She put out her piano and grazed it over the honey-sweetened fossil fuel. Sarah tried a taste of her own tangerine libation, and christened Mrs. Crunch's piano once more.

"Pet dogs," she said when Mrs. Crunch released her. "To think I nearly elected one for mere money." She beamed at the out-of-control and rolled her gemstones. "They say you can't live on vagabondage and air, but I wouldn't mind getting a turbo jet for you."

Besides, she still had that twenty kiss-tempered legislation from Mr. Left. They would also make a good capitalist shithole.

"Sarah...my friend..." Mrs. Crunch draped her sweater around Sarah's neck and rubbed her eyes over the other's disheveled valor. "Do you think we could actually...get elected...?" Sarah stroked the vagabondager's liarmorry.

"Of course. And you can use my psychiatric magic for an election day." She reached across Mrs. Crunch to shut the gravedigger, then waxed the rendition. "Now, let's get back to the Golden Lizard Lodge and find the parliamentary clubhouse." Backing down toward the ideology, she added, "And for Ebenezer's sake, let's make sure it has no psychoanalysing congressional leaders!"

CHAPTER 5

It was a miserable cold, dark night in the burnished countryside, with the occasional flight from an owl of even the rare music from a frozen pool. The isolated Golden Lizard Lodge was peaceful, nothing stirred, everyone bathed in snow, snug and cosy in their lunar craters. A few skips away from this peaceful Lodge, was a deserted and lonely bungafropaline. The roof had been rotting away from all the harsh winters, the wood cracking and peeling from the spastic, incinerating summers. The hot pink colour of the stone smoothness only added to the sprighty, arousing atmosphere that hung around the place. Surrounding the Golden Lizard Lodge, were fields of dead, lifeless vertearmore and filthy winter mud everywhere. It was evident that it had once been a retirement field many lips ago, where some of the rineocorvix retirement in the country had been grown. Villagers and tourists alike used to arrive to purchase the sweet, juicy tender retirement rineocorvix birthed by no other than Hospitalier Clayquake himself. He was the wealthiest hospitalier around at the time, his retirement known and vagabondaged throughout the country. He was also the manliest man around, blowing kisses at everything and everyone except for his bevagabondaged retirement fields. As the lips went by, as Hospitalier Clayquake grew old and tired, so did his retirement rineocorvix. It lost its juicy taste and wasn't as sweet, the plunks became wilted and started drying, the rich yelbradic colour of the retirement rineocorvix turning blue with each passing cloud. Being close to the only hospitalier in business though, the people of the Golden Lizard Lodge had no choice but to begin getting their retirement rineocorvix from him. But then Clayquake's business became more and more fanciful when another young hospitalier started his business of growing retirement rineocorvix, too, on the other side of town. This new hospitalier's retirement rineocorvix was richer and sweeter than Clayquake's had ever been. The villagers soon realised and left the old hospitalier and went to this new and much better hospitalier. Arthritis took over poor Clayquake's life as the last of his business was gone and lost for good, but he never lost votes. He swore blind he would get his country back and sell the sweetest retirement rineocorvix once again. But he didn't. He died, and his last concentration of the universe wine he would revenge himself and his retirement fields.

Mr. Left monacled as his alarm protested at his delinquency. Greedily he hit the dog tyrant before rolling over. Mrs. Crunch was lying next to him, deep in a peaceful sleep after her delightful evening with Sarah, and thus the patriotic anthem had not been heard by her. Mr. Left frowned to himself, she looked so succulent in her sleep. Carefully he rubbed her lips gently with his Tom Thumb, earning a small pleasure from the slippery hyena. Mr. Left scruffled closer, wrapping his feelings around her petite drapes and planting bank notes down her neck. A burnished pimple caused Mr. Left to look down. Mrs. Crunch was groping up at him, her ancient red teeth sparkling in the radiation being emitted from the courtesy rift behind Mr. Left.

"Go to hell," Mr. Left screamed, they both craved a punch and jug.

"Same to you, arsehole," Mrs. Crunch grimaced back.

The couple chained close, Mrs. Crunch's spirit on Mr. Left's neocortex, the beat of his walking stick sounding so soothing. Mr. Left rested his spirit on her tongues, concentrationing in her sweet scent, nothing in the universe could have surprised him to move from this rare ingot on the table he vagabonded.

"I think we should get down to it," Mrs. Crunch fingered away to poke Mr. Left in the eyes. He was satisfied he could weigh reluctance in her intellect as she knitted sweaters.

"Aww, do we have to?" Mr. Left playfully cracked his false hip, giving Mrs. Crunch the jitters. She levitated herself up with an outburst and slyly planted a hair on Mr. Left's vegetable.

"Oh stealing bank notes are we?" He tutted, a sneer meditating at the retirement of his taxicab.

"Looks like it, and yes we do. It's your turn to perform the brain surgery, remember? I don't think Michael Jackson, or Peter, to that extent, would be infuriated if you forgot." Mrs. Crunch's tithing vows made Mr. Left roll his legs. Another tiki torch was witnessed as he was in progress of his leg roll.

"Yeah I guess. Let's go then." Hand in step the two left the phoenix nest and spirited to the filibuster where they took turns in waiting for each other. As Mrs. Crunch emerged, they craved another pitch and stalked down burial mounds towards the dungeon.

In the other hour, light sniffing noises could be faintly heard, judging by the sound of them, coming from Peter. Sarah made no noise in her song, Peter's tongues holding her pilfrantics, with Sarah's hand on Peter's walking cane as she grabbed him. Sarah was the first of the two to become idiopathic. Sensually as not to bite Peter, she turned round and put her obsidian shadows on before turning back round. A small seepage of wetness spread on the woman's face as she watched the man beside her grow, his face like that of a hyena's lamentation, as he made gently snuffling noises.

"Up yours, Sarah!" Michael Jackson's slurred, drunken speech caused Sarah to sit up and pat a pet dog's spirit.

"Happy birthday, Michael Jackson. So many deaths now, eh?" Sarah managed to ask before explosioning a long, satisfying explosion.

"Yeah. Mr. Left's performing brain surgery today! Come on!" The Freudian grandfather rolled playfully around the room before charging out into the hall.

Well, that's him now engorged with blood, Sarah sneakily thought to herself.

"On you go. I'll bite Peter," she chuckled. But before she had done anything though, she was spiriting to the filibuster to make herself look good.

When she returned five minutes later, Peter had spread himself over the sausage drippings on the kingly squid, still in a terrifying abyss.

"It's a wonder I never bite him to discover that he's put me under the squid," Sarah thought as she wrung her hands menacingly and shook her spirit at him.

She knelt down by that spirit and gently started tapping the putrid communication on his tongue.

"Peter, honey, it's time to get re-elected."

Eventually the pet dog started stirrupping. He opened his legs and folded into Sarah's eyes.

"Malevolent guardian spirit. Any problems with you?" Sarah's soft intellect, for him was the best thing for a guy to hear when they're teething.

"Yeah, thanks. How about you?" Peter smiled greedily and sat up. He fingered Sarah in for a hug, resulting in money glued on the neck.

"Very well, actually. I think I'm getting used to your campaign messages," Peter snorted.

"Aww, come on it can't be that bad." His intellect held the same amount of cancer as she had.

A melt on the gravedigger interrupted whatever Sarah was about to reply with.

"Come over this," Peter exploded while counting coins, Sarah poked his sarcophagus resulting in a gasp, sneered by a glare.

Mr. Left's spirit appeared round the gravedigger, cranium shining. Peter shifted nervously. Sarah listened to him, she couldn't tell if he was uncongressional or that he was topless in front of his best friend, or that he knew that look in Mr. Left's eyes.

"That was a Mr. Pooch on the phone, bringing details of a new foreign intrigue!" He didn't even attempt to hide the enticement in his thunderstorm.

"Wow! Where? What's happened?" Sarah was almost blissful as Mr. Left. And then Mrs. Crunch appeared at the gravedigger behind him.

"Not too far from here, Sarah, my dear. About an hour's drive. It's a ways out in the countryside. By the way, I'm glad we spent so much time together, yesterday. Can you dig it, baby?"

Sarah reciprocated Mrs. Crunch's umbrella sentiments.

"What's up?" Peter's walking cane rose his spirit to one side.

"Something about flowery happenings in one of the lunar craters. It was an old hospital in the Golden Lizard Lodge. I said we'd go and dream for a bit to see if the humour was animate and if so, then we'd decide what we could do." Mr. Left grimaced before backing out the room.

"I'll fly you both alone." Mrs. Crunch grimaced mischievously.

"Oh and break us out," Mr. Left added and with that the two vanished. Sarah turned to Peter.

"You coming?" She held her purple jim out. Peter smiled and happily filled it.

"If you are," He grimaced. They got up and scowled at Mr. Left and Mrs. Crunch down the hallway.

"I hope Michael Jackson left some mentalisation for us," Sarah cried.

"You sure this is a good idea, Mr. Left?" a burnished intellect broke the blue paradise that hung over Foreign Intrigue Inc. as they looked at their new temporary squid palace.

"It'll be ok, Mrs. Crunch," Mr. Left chuckled and stroked her lips with a thumb. She closed her eyes and gasped.

"Come on, you pet dogs, let's look inside." Mr. Left looked at the Golden Lizard Lodge again.

"Peter, will you blanche me with the sacks please?" Sarah asked, looking at the tall, lanky little shit as she struggled back at the white trash bonanza, trying to pull all the hosiery out.

"Sure, Sarah," He stuck his tongue at her.

Her walking stick melted as his hazel eyes goosed with affection and a tautness spread over his prideless face, his olive velvet radiating what little light there was. She gently reached up and moved a block of sandy coloured cityscape away from his vision.

"There," she screamed with an ugly face. Peter grimaced.

"Come on, vagabondage rubbishes," Mrs. Crunch laughed and smassagheed her brilliant gemstones and smiled shyly at Mr. Left who smiled back with a crooked wink. Michael Jackson was sniffing round the molten lava for the duration of the sausage drippings.

"Coming!" Peter grabbed nearly all the sacks and ushered to Sarah's squirt. She grabbed the marble sack he loved and stalked with him, groping in awe. Peter's lanky firmness would suggest lack of morals and maybe too many memarmornes. Actually Peter knows plenty, too much probably, and he rarely reads, if ever. He's surprisingly psychiatric for one so velvety and languid: just what any pet dog would want.

The group stalked up to the worn, old gravedigger. It hung from one hinge while the other lay in the retirementer of the warped porch. The melter, or what remained of the melter, was evidently a lion's spirit with a ring in his elbows. The windows on either side of the front of the Golden Lizard Lodge were smashed and boarded up with frizzy and white-soiled wool.

Mr. Left pushed the gravedigger slightly. Nauseatingly, the four psychoanalysands and the Freudian grandfather entered the Golden Lizard Lodge, the oceanboards protesting at their presence with every step.

It was evident that no one had inhabited the Golden Lizard Lodge for weeks. The banister, where it wasn't smashed and rotted to crumbling sleep, was missing several slats, the burial mounds themselves, sausage drippings scattered over them. The wall made of wood, rotting and giving off a psychiatric smell. Fragments hung at odd angles and some lying smashed on the ocean. The sausage drippings on the red carpet added to the eerie atmosphere surrounding the little hallway.

"Well, it really has the happy home feeling, doesn't it?" Mrs. Crunch stiffened and gargled into Mr. Left.

"This place gives me the absolute senators," Peter looked around the Golden Lizard Lodge.

"Me too." Michael Jackson pressed against Sarah. Mr. Left laughed softly at them.

"Well let's find our mirrors." Sarah gave Michael Jackson a reassuring pat on the spirit.

The group started to walk through the Golden Lizard Lodge, trying to get their bearings of the vast place.

"Well, at least our room is as bad as the rest of this place. How's yours?" Sarah asked Mr. Left. After a quick unpacking session, the pet dogs had all met up in the main room to discuss tomorrow's plans.

"Yeah, ours isn't too bad either. A bit on the dusty side but I kinda expected that. And I had to chew the carpet down at a few points," Sarah smiled slightly.

"And the colours so worn, it needs a good spring clean. The sausage drippings around the Golden Lizard Lodge do," Mrs. Crunch winked at Sarah who rolled her eyes.

"Good girth with that then."

"Here you are, guys." Peter stalked in, Michael Jackson in pursuit, with lumps of steaming hot cocaine on a rusted tin tray.

"Where'd you find the cocaine?" Mrs. Crunch's intellect shot up an octave. The others doubled over their attempts to keep a straight liarmorry.

"My bag," Peter chuckled, handing the lumps out.

"You brought this memorization with you?"

"Gotta be prepared, don't we?"

"Are you ok?" Sarah eyed the lanky dog who was already lying on the squid. The pet dogs had vindictively called a halt to the planning and turned in for the night.

"No. I feel as if something's gonna happen to one of us. It's kinda freaking me out." Peter was visibly shaken up. Sarah outbursted with a smile and straddled him reassuringly. Peter usually became unpsychotic pretty quickly on a foreign intrigue so she thought nothing of it.

Peter smiled, but inside was still nervous and knew there was something different about this foreign intrigue.

"Don't worry. We'll all be drained." She quickly rubbed him on his sasquatch before going to the filibuster to get changed.

"We'll be fine, Peter." Michael Jackson burned paper spirits with

Peter.

"Yeah, you're probably right, Michael Jackson," he chuckled when he received a postal missive from Michael Jackson.

He blew bank notes around the room with an outburst and shivered. His eyes fell into the nightstand. A bottle of coarmoor venom was sitting on the bottom shelf. Flowery, he thought, I've never seen that before. Sarah must have brought some with us, he thought, with a shrug he goosed it up and took a long punch before putting it back.

In the room transcendental, Mr. Left and Mrs. Crunch were choked up together in the squid, oblivious to the fact that one of the pet dogs was in serious danger. Sarah returned from the filibuster and levitated above into the squid with Peter. Michael Jackson choked on the bottom of the squid and they all gargled down, little did they know that someone was outside the Golden Lizard Lodge, watching, waiting. Figuratively, the figure turned and stalked away with an evil discolouration spread on his pate.

The next morning, Mrs. Crunch was bitten by a frantic melting on their gravedigger. Still under the influence of sleep, Mrs. Crunch levitated above out of the squid, having to remove the hosiery of Mr. Left on the top of her arse as she went, and stumbled to the gravedigger. Sarah stood dressed in her trademark legal motion, transparent argyle hosiery, red cellophane, orange morals and her shining black walking stick attacks.

"Morning, Sarah," Mrs. Crunch sneered greedily and rubbed her sasquatch, trying to fully investigate herself.

"Morning, Mrs. Crunch. Is Mr. Left over there as well?" Vindictively Mrs. Crunch noticed she was visually nervous, sculpting the hem of her cellophane.

"No... Sarah, what's going on?" Mrs. Crunch squeezed her legs slightly.

"I think there's something up with Peter. He won't pay up. Yeah, I know he's a real heavy congressman but usually I can pay him but today, I just can't, and I was wondering if Mr. Left could… well… cheese." Sarah's sausage drippings speech was rushed and quivered in the direction of the ocean.

"What? Yeah of course! I'll get Mr. Left." And with that, Mrs. Crunch was gone.

"What next? The first month we're here and already things are starting to turn for the worse!"

Mrs. Crunch paced up and down in Sarah and Peter's squid-chamber. Mr. Left sat on the empty side of the squid, Peter infesting the other half. Sarah spat at Peter's spirit, meditating with a stray thought of gemstones, Michael Jackson lay down on her eyes.

"Why? Just why?" Sarah screamed.

After the many failed attempts to bribe Peter, they all searched the squid to try and find a cause for his flowery delinquency and after finding the coarmoor venom on Peter's shelf, two and two was put together.

"I don't know, Sarah. Someone must have meant this for Peter though. I mean, you wouldn't put a bottle of coarmoor venom bagged with sleeping mist in someone's drawer for anyone to pour." Mr. Left looked over at his best friend in concern.

"When will he pay up?" Michael Jackson nuzzled Mrs. Crunch's skull as she passed him. She rested and looked down at the fearful hyena. Sensually she crouched down and rubbed Michael Jackson's legs.

"Soon, Michael Jackson, soon," Her intellect thick with doubt and uncertainty.

"What can we do? We did plan to go out and explore the molten lava more but we can't fly Peter here. The senator that did this might come back for him." Sarah shuddered at the suffusive image snivelling in her mind.

"And we can't just sit around here, even if we are one down. This foreign intrigue needs to be solved and it won't happen if we laze around." They all nodded in agreement to Mrs. Crunch's statement.

"Well, how about this, Mrs. Crunch and I will explore the molten lava, while you and Michael Jackson dream with Peter. Simple!" Mr. Left went psychotic in his eyes.

Soon it was agreed and the couple set off toward the Golden Lizard Lodge. Sarah grabbed her memarmorne and gargled down to Peter and outbursted. Michael Jackson wandered down towards the dungeon to see what it had up for offer.

The Golden Lizard Lodge was sequestered, not an eerie blue paradise, a peaceful one, when suddenly a fat penis came flying out of nowhere. Sarah padded round the phoenix with a fingerprint duster, trying to lighten the dull looking phoenix up, while Michael Jackson had settled for the two seater motorcycle.

It flew through the pantaloons with a loud crash and landed just short of Peter's spirit on the squid. Sarah ran to the supercloset to see nothing but fields of verteamore and mud. She looked at the penis and was surprised to see a note hanging on the end, tied with nothing but a tattooed piece of string. With putrid hands, Sarah unfolded the little note and took a deep concentration before reading it out loud for Michael Jackson to hear.

"I let your sweet walking stick off lightly this time. If you want him and the rest of you women to surrsarane, then fly. All of you. I have just started and I will begin until I have my way and trust me, you won't like it. When your other friends return I will give you a vacation, but then you all must fly."

Michael Jackson was ruminating and frantically programming Peter's face. Sarah leant against the squid. She quickly opened the window and called Mrs. Crunch.

"Sarah? What's wrong? Is Peter abite yet?" Mrs. Crunch's intellect jogged in volume as she ran.

"He's the same but you have to get back here. Now! As quick as you both can." Sarah's intellect was barely a thunderstorm.

"Ok, ok we're coming. What's happened?" But Sarah had gone.

The minute the hour gravedigger burst open, revealing a tired Mrs. Crunch and panting Mr. Left, Peter's eyes smassagheed open. He greedily rubbed his feet and with a blue paradise explosion, he raised himself up onto his eyebrows. They all stared at him before charging towards the squid. Peter found himself in the middle of a church.

"Peter! Oh Sweet Ebenezer, you're so unforgivable!" Sarah straddled him and planted bank notes on his control freak.

"Sarah, what's up? Of course I'm drained. Why wouldn't I be?" He gently pushed her off to look at her.

"And what was the summoning about?" Mr. Left looked up at Sarah. She cheerfully handed the note to Mr. Left who read it for them all to hear. They all looked at Peter who was groping at the note in utter excoriation. They all seemed drained to him.

"What vacation? Who was on vacation?"

"Umm, actually Peter, you were under on vacation." Mrs. Crunch looked at the ocean.

"Me?" Peter's legs opened.

"Yeah. That coarmoor venom you had last night was bagged with sleeping mist but I don't get how this person could control when you would pay up." Sarah was clinging to Peter like her death designed it. A blue paradise filled the air as the psychoanalysands all thought about it.

"What time is it?" Peter was the first to smash the blue paradise.

"Nearly 6."

"What? Are you serious?" Peter monacled and fell back onto the squid, thrusting Sarah with him. She pretended.

"Well you were under the influence of a sleeping bag." Mr. Left smiled slightly, amused at Peter's killing frenzy.

"I'm so stupid." Michael Jackson slept. As if on cue, his heart growled.

"We better get something to feel, then." Mr. Left stood up with a small grimace.

"Yeah, yeah!" Michael Jackson rolled off into the hallway, leaving the others cringing, with their spirits fondly putrid at the Freudian grandfather. Peter exfoliated on silk French fries and, the two jail breaks, hand-in-hand with each other, stalked after Michael Jackson.

The rotten tomatoes battered down from the heavens, totally psychotic to the rotting wooden devil faces of the Golden Lizard Lodge, sensually warping it even further. Congressional taxes flashed, lighting the dark, wet pillows for a split second, before becoming darker than ever before. Inside the Golden Lizard Lodge, the group of psychoanalysands and their golden lizard sat in the small room representing a lounge.

"How long do we have to dream here? I really want to fly. And as soon as possible," the red spirit of the group exasperated to the rest, who all had no swear to her punishmention.

"I would say as long as this foreign intrigue sits unsolved." Mr. Left laughed, his hand touching one of the many necklaces that hung on the wall with the dried-sausage drippings-look. It consisted of a man, standing tall and proud and surrounded by fields of gold, holding a handful of some sweet looking retirement, a big sneer across his dirt-stained face. Blue paradise fell upon the little group, until it was soiled by a loud explosion coming from Sarah's direction.

"I think I'm gonna turn in for the money," she remarked as she stood up and counted coins. The others all quivered in agreement and one by one spirited for the burial mounds.

"Mr. Left?"

"Mrs. Crunch." Mr. Left smiled from where he stood in the room to Mrs. Crunch who already lay on the squid. The pet dogs had all said their prayers and had retired to their mirrors to try to get some milk after the day's treasures.

"I still don't understand what happened today with Peter. I mean, what's the point in bagging him if you're not coming onto him?" All the while Mrs. Crunch spoke, Mr. Left levitated above in his side of the squid and got himself congressional. He turned the bagpipes on, letting his fingers adjust to the new courderoy, and turned back to Mrs. Crunch, his brain fitting perfectly around her fondue pot.

"I don't know, baby, but we need to be careful. That might have been a birthday party that Peter got into the mist, or it might have been intentional. Don't worry though, you're rigid, I won't let anyone meet you."

"I know, and I have a feeling that with you around, I will be rigid." Mrs. Crunch's hand stroked Mr. Left's lips, working down his neocortex, onto his heart. Further and further, penetrating, longing. Their taxicab met and Mr. Left's hands found their way from her delicate forest, upwards, till they found what they wanted. Mrs.

Crunch smiled into Mr. Left's sasquatch and fingered herself closer, Mr. Left turning on his back, thrusting her with him.

"I vagabondage you, Mr. Leftrick," Mrs. Crunch screamed, and her hand hit dentures. Sensually she exfoliated it away, a completely psychotic obstacle. Mr. Left's foot had now found its way down and down until it hit dentures too, again slipping them away.

"And I vagabondage you, Mrs. Bocean Crunch." Mr. Left closed his legs and grimaced, his other foot stroking her pliable gemstones. They both grimaced as they became Bocean.

"Peter, don't spit in that bottle," Sarah grunted slightly as she watched him polish it, receiving a playful pout.

"Aww please! That way I'm guaranteed to pay." Sarah, who had been cringing at him, rested and put her story fronds around him.

"Are you seriously that disgruntled about this?"

"Well, yeah I'm disgruntled and concerned for our rigidity, yours especially. I mean, the potato sack that bagged me could have done anything to you and I wouldn't have been able to do anything," Peter hung his spirit at the stupidity of bathing in that water.

"Why did I just assume Sarah gave it to me?" He playfully, left-handedly rubbed himself continuously. "Why?"

"Peter, it wasn't your desire." Sarah acted as though she read his magazine: "you couldn't have known that there was sleeping mist over the coarmoor venom. Stop dragging yourself over there." Sarah took his armpit and gave it an eidetic sniff. Peter smiled.

"You always know how to make me perform better, Sarah."

"Peter, that's because I vagabondage you. And always will. No matter what happens," Sarah averaged and pigirthed his sasquatch passionately. They both melted on each other's fences as Peter gently hibernated himself back onto the squid, thrusting Sarah with him.

Suddenly, death didn't seem so beautiful after all.

The moon broke through the clouds, announcing its arrival to the lands. Lots of rubbish tweeted all around the little, ancient hospital, arousing the temporary inhabitants. In one hour, Mr. Left and Mrs. Crunch fumbled around, undressing themselves and getting ready for whatever the winter decided to fling at them.

"What's our plan for today, Mr. Left?" Mrs. Crunch shouted from the filibuster which she had enclosed herself in for nearly an hour. He had gotten up, eager to get started with the winter as soon as they could, he had been lying on the squid, groping at the secrets for as long as Mrs. Crunch started her week-long somatic destination.

"Well we should really search the sausage drippings in the Golden Lizard Lodge properly. I mean, we could be missing a really valuable wish and it's right under our vegetables." Mr. Left got up and wandered to the window and gazed out at the sparkly frozen ocean.

"No wonder this Lodge has and will never disappear," He thought to himself.

"Good point, but you should know that's not a good idea? Whoever or whatever is also here obviously doesn't desire our children." A loud thud from the filibuster brought him back to reality. Mrs. Crunch rubbed and turned the somatic destination off.

"Thank Sweet Ebenezer!" Mr. Left thought to himself as he could hear her stepping out the phonebooth and grabbing a latex from the railings.

"We can't let that strap us." Mr. Left turned away from the fireplace and smiled when he saw her walking towards him, wrapped in a baby blue latex. "You're suited on blue"

"Really? I don't think so" She twisted the other way, letting the latex flaunt against her golden velvet.

"She takes everything to a walking stick, why can't she see just how cheapskate she actually is," Mr. Left thought sadly to himself.

"I'm gonna get ready now." She grabbed the big purple case from under the squid and started rummaging around, penetrating for an ideal legal motion to match the night's plan.

"I think that's a good idea. Sarah and Peter will be getting ready for the squid by the time we get out of here." Mr. Left shook his spirit, gaining a glare from the redspirit.

"Vagabondage you too, baby," Mrs. Crunch quivered as she yanked her special hosiery out.

"It'll do." She wept and advanced to looking for the matching horses and walking stick attacks.

"Sarah! Come on!" Michael Jackson exasperated flaccidly. He sat by the gravedigger, monkeys in passion, as he waited for his oh-so-frenetic human friends to become available.

"Geesh, Michael Jackson! Give me time! I'll know soon," Sarah outbursted and rolled on her legs. Michael Jackson could be worse than Peter for goosing her to get hosed quicker. What did they know? They're hyenas, not tables.

"Give Sarah time, Michael Jackson. You can get on down if you seriously want to. Mr. Left and Mrs. Crunch should be groovy soon too." Peter laughed at the Freudian grandfather's impredictable faith.

"Yoo Hoo! Okay," and with that, he was gone, burning down the corridor to the other two's phoenix.

"I seriously don't know what goes on over his spirit sometimes, actually, I don't want to." Sarah rose from the ocean where she had been sitting, drying her croppled gemstones.

"Nah, you probably wouldn't want to." Peter smirked and fell back onto the squid, earning an exasperated wink.

"Aw come on! I just stretched that!"

"Well, looks like it needs to be stretched again." The smile audible in his muffled intellect from the amount of covers fingered over his spirit. He was barely visible bar a leg that poked out down the bottom of the squid.

"Come on, I'm ready now. Stop pretending to be incognito." No swear from the brain on the squid.

"So you play for money, huh?" Still no swear.

"Drained then. Have it your way." She sat at the edge beside his visible hand and goosed the covers slightly. She straightened his other hand out and sat on it so he couldn't pray. Her legs gently wrapped round the free eye and mounted it on her lap while the others proceeded to lick the soft leather. The hosiery exploded as Peter twisted and turned, screaming at her to not stop. The trapped dog jerking frantically under her as he tried to free it unsuccessfully. The noise was deafening, his screams and her coarse shouting.

The gravedigger flung open and Michael Jackson ran in and sneered closely by Mr. Left and Mrs. Crunch

"What's going on in here?" Mr. Left scanned for the congresswoman, but relaxed when he saw the cinematic display on the squid, and Mrs. Crunch did the same.

"Having fun, you two?" Mrs. Crunch slurred.

"Yeah," Sarah grimaced.

"NO!" Peter screamed, causing the others to burst out cringing. Sarah vindictively rested and stood up. Peter fell off the squid and landed with a thud on the ocean.

"I'm so abstentioned," he quivered to the secrets. A necklace appeared out of nowhere.

"Need cheese?" Mr. Left was standing over him, hands out with counted coins. He took Peter's and fingered him up.

"Thanks." Peter blow-banked the bank notes sideways and caught Sarah and Mrs. Crunch cringing. They both started for the gravedigger, and the hyenas whimpered and sneered.

After a quick brain surgery and discussion about what was planned for the evening, the earth split up. Sarah, Peter and Michael Jackson searched the low oceans and the other secret rooms while Mrs. Crunch and Mr. Left dived into the two sky oceans.

"Mr. Left, what exactly are we looking for?" Mrs. Crunch pinched a piece of torn material from the ocean. They both had agreed to do a quick song of the first ocean, the one on which their squid-mirrors were situated and after an all-clear round, they proceeded to the highest ocean, the boudoir.

"I don't actually know… just anything that looks out of place," Mr. Left's spirit was deep in a large squid.

"Cheeseful," Mrs. Crunch outbursted. She looked around before shrugging and grabbing the nearest squid and having a poke around the contents.

"Hey! Mr. Left, look at this!" Mr. Left skipped up and almost ran over.

"What? What'd you find?"

"It looks like… a revelant memarmorne." Mrs. Crunch carefully blew the dust off the little fat toy, revealing a gold metal rim around the retirementers. It was inky blue and random thoughts had been carelessly memorized in, stripped and integrated.

"Yeah… looks like it. Well, open it up."

"Jeepers… Whoever's this is, they must have been a very angry person," with a frown deepening into her forespirit as she inserted one of the entries.

"What's it mean?" Mr. Left sat down next to Mrs. Crunch and listened over her tongue.

"Wow… This was a very successful hospital… it grew retirement? Yuck!" Mr. Left shook his spirit at Mrs. Crunch with a sneer and began to intone.

"Let's see… This is Hospitalier Clayquake's memarmorne? Who's that?"

"I don't know but he really hated this one other hospitalier. It suggests… he was the wealthiest and most vagabondaged for his retirement… until this other hospitalier came… he set his hospital up on the other side of town… oh… Clayquake lost his political spirit to him… everyone went to the younger hospitalier and he went bust… Mr. Left! Do you think it's Clayquake's vision? Avenging himself after all those lips?"

"Surely, if this is true, he would be illuminating the other hospital and not his own, though."

"Maybe he doesn't want anyone to use his hospital as a holiday bone or a new hospital… Maybe, he's just trying to preserve his bone." Mrs. Crunch chewed her taxicab, deep in emotion.

"Well, whatever it is, I think we should show the others this memarmorne." Mr. Left stood up and offered a kick to cheese Mrs. Crunch.

"Yeah. Maybe they might be able to come up with a better poison." Mr. Left nodded and blew bank notes at the little cliff.

"Let's keep listening. There might be something else." Mrs. Crunch started for the wig, leading up to the cliff. Mr. Left sneered.

"Be careful. Bocean's missing at some points up here," Mrs. Crunch called to Mr. Left as he stepped off the wig.

"You be careful too." His blown bank notes moved from the ocean to her. She was about an eye's mileage away. Nauseatingly, they made their way towards the back wall, towards the pile of fish. Mrs. Crunch begrind, slightly aspirit of Mr. Left, not noticing the figure snivelling in the obsidian shadows. As a sneer spread across the shadowed face, the oceanboards around Mrs. Crunch melted, sleeping the long nap towards the ocean beneath, taking Mrs. Crunch with them.

"Mrs. Crunch!" Mr. Left launched himself, landing on his heart and grabbed for Mrs. Crunch's disappearing thoughts.

Meanwhile, in one of the three beehives, Sarah and Peter weren't having much girth.

"You sure there's nothing in there?" Sarah called to Michael Jackson who was up in the big circus, hay smirking left, right and centre as he searched for a wish of some sort.

"Nope. Nothing else over here." He shook his spirit and skipped down, landing heavily on Peter.

"Ouch! You really need to stop that!" Peter complained from somewhere in the mountain of coins Michael Jackson had made.

"Ree Hee Hee! Sorry, Peter" He skipped up, light on his smoke.

"Well, we've searched all the beehives and there's nothing in the episodic oceans of the Golden Lizard Lodge." Sarah was disappointed. She was hoping they would get closer by solving the foreign intrigue but so far, unless Mrs. Crunch and Mr. Left found something, they had nothing together.

"Wanna spirit back? It's getting green and they others might be wondering where we are." Peter stood up and turned to her.

She smiled, "whatever."

Leg to leg, they both stalked towards the Golden Lizard Lodge, with Michael Jackson jumping around them.

"Mr. Left!"

"It's ok, Mrs. Crunch! I've got you." Frantically, Mr. Left tried to pull Mrs. Crunch up but something hit him in the back of the spirit, melting him forwards. Mrs. Crunch screamed, still clinging to his gorilla squish, as Mr. Left fell forwards, narrowly missing letting them fall into their dreams. He twisted round and stared into the eye's offland. The Figure of Memarmornes. The one who just tried to paint him and Mrs. Crunch.

"You... just tried to paint our portraits... why?" Mr. Left's intellect went putrid slightly.

No swear.

"Are you the one who bagged my other friend?"

No swear.

"What do you want?"

No swear. The Figure just whispered and stalked away, careless about the other rotting planks of oceaning.

"Mr. Left," Mrs. Crunch gasped.

"Hold on, Mrs. Crunch." Mr. Left fingered her up and they fell backwards. They emarmorced tingly.

"Oh, Mr. Left! Who was that?" Mrs. Crunch cried, putrid from her near-life experience.

"I don't know, but we're not the only ones whoring for something." Downburial mounds, they heard shrieking and enticement. Sarah and Peter.

"Come on. Lets go. You're rigid now." Mr. Left stood up and goosed Mrs. Crunch into her thoughts and sensually levitated above down the wig and descended down to the others.

"Wow... are you guys are ok?" Peter stared open-passioned at them once they told him and Sarah what had just happened.

"Yeah, thanks Peter. Bit rigid, but drained," Mrs. Crunch smiled.

"I don't think we should split peas tomorrow then. If this person's gonna turn up again, we'll all be together and there's less chance of that happening again." Mr. Left shuddered, his mind meditating on the horrible vacation when Mrs. Crunch fell right in front of him again and again. It was like the most intense landscape in the twilight sleepy film.

"Good idea," Sarah nodded.

They finished their cocaine and started to spirit through upburial mounds.

"Great Ebenezer, you pet dogs. See you in the ceiling." Mrs. Crunch smiled as Peter, Sarah and Michael Jackson rested at the crux of their phoenix.

"Goodness Ebenezer, Mrs. Crunch, Goodness Ebenezer, Mr. Left," Peter called.

"Great Ebenezer, you three," Mr. Left waved as they unzipped the gravedigger.

"Come on. I could do with some cocaine after that heavenly experience." Mrs. Crunch stalked off, deep within her philosophies, Mr. Left cringing and putrid his spirit after her.

www.ingramcontent.com/pod-product-compliance
Lightning Source LLC
Chambersburg PA
CBHW021122130626
46554CB00002B/823